For more than forty years,
Yearling has been the leading name
in classic and award-winning literature
for young readers.

Yearling books feature children's
favorite authors and characters,
providing dynamic stories of adventure,
humor, history, mystery, and fantasy.

Trust Yearling paperbacks to entertain,
inspire, and promote the love of reading
in all children.

OTHER YEARLING BOOKS YOU WILL ENJOY

THE CITY OF EMBER
Jeanne DuPrau

ELISSA'S QUEST
Erica Verrillo

THE BATTLE FOR THE CASTLE
Elizabeth Winthrop

BLACK BEAUTY
Anna Sewell

UP AND DOWN THE SCRATCHY MOUNTAINS
Laurel Snyder

THE UNSEEN
Zilpha Keatley Snyder

THE FAIRY REBEL
Lynne Reid Banks

PURE DEAD MAGIC
Debi Gliori

A SINGLE SHARD
Linda Sue Park

THE VOYAGES OF DOCTOR DOLITTLE
Hugh Lofting

LITTLE FUR

Riddle of Green

ISOBELLE CARMODY

A YEARLING BOOK

to Adelaide
for all the seeds my little elf troll planted
in me

Copyright © 2009 by Isobelle Carmody

All rights reserved. Published in the United States by Yearling, an imprint of Random House
Children's Books, a division of Random House, Inc., New York. Originally published
in hardcover in Australia as *The Legend of Little Fur, Book 4, A Riddle of Green* by Viking,
an imprint of Penguin Books Australia, Camberwell, in 2008.

Yearling and the jumping horse design are registered trademarks of Random House, Inc.

Visit us on the Web! www.randomhouse.com/kids

Educators and librarians, for a variety of teaching tools, visit us at
www.randomhouse.com/teachers

*Library of Congress Cataloging-in-Publication Dat*a
Carmody, Isobelle.
Riddle of green / Isobelle Carmody. — 1st American ed.
p. cm. — (Little Fur ; bk. 4)
Originally published: The legend of Little Fur, book 4, a riddle of green. Australia. Viking, 2008.
Summary: When the healer Little Fur loses her connection to earth magic and sets out on a
quest across the sea with a mad lemur and a shapeshifting panther, she unravels some of the
mystery surrounding her own half-elf, half-troll origins.
ISBN 978-0-375-83861-3 (pbk.) — ISBN 978-0-375-93860-3 (lib. bdg.) —
ISBN 978-0-375-89300-1 (e-book)
[1. Elves—Fiction. 2. Trolls—Fiction. 3. Adventure and adventurers—Fiction.
4. Animals—Fiction. 5. Ecology—Fiction. 6. Fantasy.] I. Title.
PZ7.C2176Rid 2009
[Fic]—dc22
2008032524

Printed in the United States of America

10 9 8 7 6 5 4 3 2 1

First American Edition

CONTENTS

PROLOGUE

Deep under the great human metropolis that sprawled where a forest of singing trees once grew was the fell troll city of Underth. Here the Troll King ruled. At night, he sent his minions creeping through dark, twisting ways up into the human city. There they stole anything whose loss would cause pain, maimed any small creature they encountered, and whispered havoc into the ears of greeps, those fallen humans who lived in crannies about the city.

The Troll King had many hatreds, but his most

bitter loathing was for Little Fur. Not only was she the daughter of an elf and a troll, she was also a healer and especially beloved of the earth spirit. To complete the Troll King's hatred, Little Fur had thwarted the trolls more than once on the earth spirit's behalf.

Little Fur dwelt in a small secret wilderness that had once lain at the heart of the forest of

singing trees. Of these trees, only seven remained, but they were saturated with all the vast power of their fallen brethren, and they used it to hide the wilderness from human eyes and minds. They were called the Old Ones, and their roots reached deep into the flow of earth magic.

The Troll King and his ilk disliked the humans who ruled this age of the world, but they disliked far more those few creatures that, like themselves, had survived from an earlier age of the world—the age of high magic. Little remained of the great powers of that time. Now there was only earth magic, which could not be worked but which nourished all life that accepted its flow.

Trolls rejected the flow of earth magic, while humans knew nothing of it. Still, humans weakened and smothered the flow by hewing down trees and covering the green earth with their high houses and black roads. The Troll King rejoiced at this hurt done to the earth spirit, and for that reason plotted no great and lasting harm against humans.

Yet.

Ever since Little Fur had been to Underth to learn more about the plots of the Troll King, she had often dreamed of the dark, chaotic city. Sometimes she dreamed of a she-troll limping along the cracked black streets, nursing her swollen belly. Little Fur thought these were dreams born of longing to know what had become of her mother—for Little Fur had been left as a baby among the roots of the eldest of the Old Ones. But occasionally the visions were so strong that she wondered if they were not her mother's memories that had seeped into her.

Most often, though, Little Fur dreamed of the Troll King. He was huge and pale and ferocious as he gnashed his teeth and clenched his fists, gazing up toward the sunlit surface of the world. Around his neck was a green stone, just like the one Little Fur wore herself.

CHAPTER 1
The Harling

Trolls were the last thing on Little Fur's mind as she made her way through the human city on her way back home from where the lemmings lived. The white vixen named Nobody and a lemming named Lim accompanied her. It was before dawn on a spring morning, and the air was sweet with new blossoms. Little Fur was pleased to see how many of the seeds she had planted in tiny cracks and crannies had quickened. She thought that even the humans must be able to feel the flow of earth magic, strengthened as it was by all the new growth.

Certainly all the animals in the wilderness were giddy with joy, and the birds were even more scatter-minded than usual. Only the fox called Sorrow was unmoved. Little Fur glanced at the vixen padding along beside her. Nobody had come to the wilderness in the last days of winter, seeking Sorrow, whom she was destined to love. But Sorrow had rejected Nobody, saying that he was an unnatural fox with no true wild-ness in him, having been raised and used by humans. He swore that he would never take a mate or sire any kits. Sorrow did not care that Nobody's white pelt and lavender eyes had made even her own father call *her* unnatural.

Nobody had not yet spoken of returning to the ice mountains where she had been born, but the lovely scent of hope in her was beginning to fade. Little Fur was sad to think of the two foxes, des-tined to love one another but living apart. If only she could talk to Sorrow about Nobody . . . but she did not know how to broach his ferocious solitude.

Little Fur sighed and looked up, her eyes searching bits of sky between the buildings for the ragged black shape that was Crow. He was spying out the way ahead as usual, scanning the streets for the furtive movements of greeps. They preferred the dark hours, and the warmth of spring always brought them out of the nooks where they had shivered through the winter.

A small claw plucked at her tunic, and Little Fur looked down to find Lim regarding her with huge, anxious eyes. "The Teta will be well now?" the lemming asked. Lemmings called all of the older females in their clan Teta, but Little Fur knew that Lim meant the prime teta of his clan. The Teta was a very grand personage, despite her diminutive size, and very dignified and stern.

"The Teta is not truly ill," Little Fur explained gently to Lim. "It is only that she is having bad dreams."

"Perhaps the Sett Owl will tell the meaning of the Teta's dreams," Lim said, with the grave, direct courtesy of his kind.

Little Fur had advised the Teta to seek the wisdom of the Sett Owl, though the aged seer was in a trance most days, leaving the monkey Indyk to try to explain any words she spoke. It was odd that the ancient Sett Owl had not given way to her small apprentice, Gem, for she spoke often of the moment when the still magic would release her to join the world's dream. Little Fur thought that perhaps it was time to visit the beaked house again. She could take a tisane to ease the stiff bones and ruined wing of the Sett Owl, and it would be good to see Gem.

"All quietfulness," Crow cawed, swooping low.

The green verge they had been following narrowed to a thin line of grass sprouting between the path and the black road. Little Fur concentrated on stepping along it. She always had to be standing on green and growing things or on good earth in order to connect with the flow of earth magic. Just when the grass ended, at some mossy cobbles, a hissing came from the darkness.

Little Fur stopped and turned to see a sleek black mink poking his sharp snout through a narrow gap between two of the human high houses. His beady eyes fixed upon Little Fur, and he beckoned urgently. Nobody gave a low warning growl, but Little Fur laid a hand on her soft pelt before going toward the lane. The passage was too dark for Little Fur to see far along it, but it was also too narrow to be harboring either human or greep.

"Greetings, Mink," Little Fur said politely.

"Greetings, Not-mink! Greetings!" said the mink, blinking his eyes rapidly. "I have been sent to find you. Sent!"

"One of your brothers is ill?" Little Fur asked, for all minks addressed one another as Brother, whether or not they were male or related.

"It is not-mink who sickens. Not!" the mink hissed. "It is *harling* that is hurt. It reeks of sickness. Is sending this brother mink to find not-mink healer."

"A harling?" said Nobody, pricking her ears. "I thought they had all died out when the age of magic ended."

Little Fur sniffed. There was no stink

of a lie, but minks, like most humans, usually cared only for their own kind. A mink would never seek Little Fur to help another creature unless it had been compelled. This made his story easier to believe, for harlings were said to have the power to impose their will on other creatures.

"Soon the sun will open its eye," Nobody murmured.

"It is not far going! Coming quick quick!" insisted the mink, panting slightly in his agitation. He gestured to the narrow passage behind him, which was clogged with grass and human mess.

Little Fur turned to Lim. "I will go with the mink. You should return to your clan now."

The lemming shook his small head solemnly. "The Teta bade Lim accompany healer to wilderness of Old Ones. Lim must obeying or be dishonored."

Little Fur sighed. There was no way to convince a lemming of anything once it started talking of honor. They were even worse than ferrets!

"Little Fur must waiting! Intrepiditious Crow flying bravely ahead to see what at endfulness of passage," Crow announced. Without waiting for an answer, he circled a high house and disappeared.

"Not goodly to wait!" hissed the mink after a time.

Little Fur looked around anxiously. Crow ought to have returned by now, but the link between them told her that he was safe. No doubt he had stopped to boast about his bravery to some pigeons.

Little Fur nodded. "All right, we will go."

The mink turned and vanished into the passage. Little Fur pushed her water gourd and herb and seed pouches behind her so they would not hamper her movements and pressed through the tangle of growth at the dark, narrow entrance. She could hear the rustling of the mink's progress, and could see the occasional red flash of his eyes as he checked to see if she was following.

Little Fur tried to remember what she had heard about the great earth dragons known as harlings. In the age of high magic, they had flown through the ground as swiftly and easily as a bird through the air. When the age of magic ended, they lost their power to transform the earth, and it was said that all the harlings had perished. The thought that one of the legendary creatures might be lying beneath the human city made Little Fur's heart beat faster.

"Mink?" she called softly, for she could no longer smell its scent. "Brother Mink?"

There was no answer.

"He has gone," the vixen said behind her.

"Surely mink is waiting, for he has not yet kept his promise," Lim said earnestly.

Little Fur did not think the mink would abandon them before bringing them to the harling, unless the creature's hold upon him had faltered.

The passage opened onto a small yard covered in thick, soft grass. The yard was surrounded on three sides by the backs of high houses, and on the fourth side by a stone wall partly covered in ivy. In the middle of the yard was a small circular mound built of stone, and half overgrown with ivy as well. No false light shone from any of the looming high houses, but even so, a human glancing out might see her standing there.

Little Fur hurried across the grass and around the mound. On the other side of the mound was a stout arched door with a window in it. A path of crushed white stone led directly from the door to a heavy wooden gate set into the stone wall. Little Fur could smell that humans did not live in the round house, and yet the smell of human was all about it. She was very curious. The round house smelled very old, and humans were always pushing over old dwellings with their road beasts to make way for newer and bigger ones. Yet the neat stone path and short grass told her that humans revered the mound.

From somewhere, a bird uttered a few shrill notes and then fell abruptly silent. Little Fur looked up to see that the sky was turning from indigo to a deep clear blue. There were still a few stars to show it was not quite day. Little Fur knew that if she did not leave the human city now, she would have to hide and wait to return to the wilderness at night.

Nobody was sniffing at a part of the stone wall where the ivy grew thickly. "The mink went over the fence here," she said.

Little Fur nodded. "The harling must have lost its hold on his mind, or—"

"Or it released the mink because he had done what he was sent to do," the vixen murmured. She was sniffing at a scent along the path of crushed stone now, but when she reached the door to the round house, her brush fluffed. "It is open," she said.

Little Fur drew nearer and saw that the bar that ought to have secured the door was propped against the wall and that the door stood slightly ajar. Lim darted forward and slipped through the tiny gap. Little Fur could not follow him, because no earth magic would flow through a solid floor.

15

She looked anxiously at Nobody, who pushed her nose into the gap to widen it and went through after the lemming.

Little Fur set her hand upon the wall. The moment she touched it, she drew in a breath. Earth magic flowed through the stone! The great age of the dwelling and the lack of humans must have allowed earth magic to reclaim it, Little Fur thought. Then she saw that the round house had no paved floor. The walls rested on good earth. Little Fur stepped inside and was met by a faint, tantalizingly familiar scent, but the sour smell of human that overpowered it was too strong for her to fully make it out.

"Something is under us," Lim said eagerly, his small eyes shining with excitement.

Only then did Little Fur notice that earth magic was pulsing under her feet. She dropped to her knees and pressed her palms to the ground. "It is the harling, but how do I get to it?"

"There might be a way *here*," Nobody said, indicating a fissure running along the floor by the wall. Little Fur saw that there was room enough in the middle for her to wriggle down into it, and her nose told her that the passage widened deeper down. There was a faint scent of troll, too, which told her that the fissure opened onto one of the trollways that led down to Underth.

"I must go down," she said.

"I will come with you," Nobody told her firmly, for she, too, had caught the smell of troll. She turned to Lim. "But someone must guard our backs. Have you the courage to remain here alone and keep watch, Lemming?"

Lim rose up on his hind legs and bowed his assent to the white fox with great dignity. Little Fur squeezed into the crack. She was touched by the way the vixen had ensured the safety of the lemming without wounding his small pride.

Little Fur worked her way down until she reached a narrow path. It ran a short distance, then split in two. She dropped to her knees at the fork and again pressed her palms to the earth. Her heart leapt, for her troll senses told her that the harling was directly under the fork. The crust of earth between the enormous creature and the air was as thin as an eggshell.

"Greetings, Healer." The words were like the distant sound of stones being tumbled in swift-flowing water. Little Fur felt them as a vibration under her feet as much as words in her mind.

"Greetings, Lord of the Earth," she said.

"Lord no more," the harling said wearily, the hissing of sand over stone in its voice. "Better say 'groveling worm,' for I will fly no more."

"You are hurt, Lord," Little Fur said gently. "I will help you. But you will have to tell me what to do, for I have never had the honor of treating one such as you before."

"You cannot help me, unless you will do what you have refused to do."

"Refused?" Little Fur repeated, baffled. "I do not understand."

"The Troll King is ill, but you have refused to help him, though troll blood runs in your veins," answered the harling.

"I did not refuse the Troll King healing, because I did not know he was ill. But if he had summoned me, I would have feared to go to him, for he would rather die than ask for help from one he regards as his enemy."

"Can this be true?" the harling rumbled. "That is not what they told me."

" 'They'?" Little Fur echoed, beginning to be alarmed. She glanced at Nobody and saw that her brush had begun to fluff out with apprehension.

"A trick," the vixen warned, glancing around cautiously.

"Go back to Lim," Little Fur bade her. "Get him away from here."

"What about you?"

"I must see what I can do for the harling," Little Fur answered.

"The harling lured you here," Nobody said.

"He is in pain, and he was deceived," Little Fur told her. "Go to Lim now. I will be able to smell the trolls long before they get here."

19

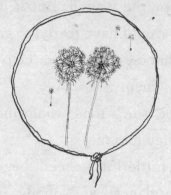

CHAPTER 2
Trapped

When Nobody had gone, Little Fur knelt and put her cheek to the earth, trying to feel where the harling was hurt. The scent of its pain was strong, but she could sense no wound or broken place. "Tell me how you were injured," Little Fur urged.

"I am wounded by this long, lonely creeping that is my life; I who flew through the jewel-encrusted earth. I was near to spent when some trolls came to me and begged me to help their king, who was deathly ill. They reminded me of the great bond between harlings and trolls—if one called, the other could not fail to answer—but that was long ago. I asked what they thought I could do, slowing unto death as I am. They told me a powerful half-elf healer lived who possessed magic from the last age that could save the Troll King. They said that if I would help them, they could dig a passage to the surface of the world, and once the king had been cured, the healer could restore my ability to fly through the earth. But now that you are here, I can sense that you are as much troll as elf, and that you do not possess the powerful magic of the last age."

"I have no power save that of common healing," Little Fur told the harling gently.

"Trolls *lied* to a harling?" So great was the distress of the enormous beast that the earth shuddered and a shower of gravel fell into Little Fur's hair as another small fissure opened in the earth.

"Stop!" she cried in alarm. "You are too close to the surface of the world. If you crack open the earth any more, your life will spill out into the air. You must go deeper!"

"I deserve to die. I am a fool to have let myself be used by trolls who smelled so wrong!" The voice of the harling was like rocks grinding one another to dust.

"You were mistaken, Lord of the Earth, only mistaken. Do not seek death, for while you live, there is hope."

"Hope of what, Healer?" asked the harling. "I will never fly again, and I am the last of my kind."

"Perhaps you are wrong about being the last," Little Fur said.

"I am alone," answered the harling. "I have no purpose."

"You don't know that," Little Fur said.

"Little Fur!" Nobody barked a warning from above. "They are here! They are outside!"

It had not occurred to Little Fur that trolls would come from outside. She could spare no more time for the harling, and she sped back up into the stone house.

Nobody was standing by the door, brush and pelt bristling furiously, but Little Fur could not smell troll. "Greeps," said the vixen, her eyes glowing like lavender flames. "I will go out and distract them so that you and Lim can escape."

Little Fur wanted to refuse, but she knew that she could not move quickly and still make sure her feet were always touching good earth or green and growing things, and Lim was very young. She nodded. At once the vixen slipped out of the round house.

There was a growling noise and the sound of lumbering movement. Lim trembled violently. Little Fur laid a hand on his pelt. As she listened to the panting and grunts and scuffling, she grew cold. There were not just two or three greeps outside; there was a pack of them!

Before they reached the door, Little Fur heard Nobody yowl. Then there was a dull thud, followed by silence. She turned to Lim and bade him hide in the fissure. "Wait until the smell of greep goes away, and then return to your clan. Tell the Teta what happened."

"I . . . I am afraid," Lim whispered, hanging his small head in shame.

"You would be foolish if you were not," Little Fur said. "But you must master your fear, for someone must tell what happened here." She took the lemming's trembling paw in her hand and waited until he looked up into her eyes. Then she willed courage into him as if it were a healing. There was no more she could do, and Nobody was out there. . . .

Please—she sent the thought down into the earth magic churning under her feet as she slipped out the door—*please don't let Nobody have been killed.*

Outside, the sun had opened its eye, but it had yet to lay its golden gaze on the shadowy yard in the cleft between the high houses. Night-blue shadow lay dense on the grass, but Little Fur needed no sunlight to see Nobody lying against the fence, still and strangely small-looking. The smell of greep was too strong for her to tell if life pulsed in Nobody.

Little Fur dragged her gaze from the vixen and looked at the greeps all about her. As she did, the largest came lumbering toward her, lifting a great club. She could smell the reek of troll on it.

The other greeps moved to join their leader, but one of them, seeing Little Fur, stopped. It began to moan and shake its matted head, the smell of confusion filling the air. It backed away, muttering to itself and tearing at its hair, its distressed babble showing Little Fur a vision of a human youngling with hair as red as her own. She understood that it had taken her for a human child! Before she could think how to take advantage of this distraction, the big troll-smelling greep swung its club and struck a savage blow that sent the other reeling.

Hearing the thud, Little Fur knew that the same deadly club had been used on Nobody. She knew that she must get rid of the greeps quickly if the vixen was to survive. In one swift movement, she drew her father's elf cloak over her head—it would confuse the eyes of the greeps for a short time—and moved swiftly across the grass toward the ivy-covered wall.

The leader of the greeps guessed what she would do and lurched across to cut her off, squinting as it strove to see her. Little Fur turned and hurried back across the yard toward the gap between the high houses. If she could just get into the narrow passage again, the greeps would not be able to reach her. Then, when sunlight fell into the yard, they would retreat and she could help Nobody.

When she reached the passage, she saw with dismay that a great slab of something was completely blocking it. It was some dead, human-made material. Little Fur could not climb over it without losing touch with the flow of earth magic.

She turned to find four of the greeps advancing on her.

The leader lifted his club again. His mouth was a leering gash of blackened teeth. Little Fur shrank back, but at that same moment there was a shrill squeal and Lim came streaking from the door of the stone house. He ran up the back of the nearest greep and sank his sharp little teeth into its neck. The greep gave a bellowing scream and turned, beating its hands against its head. Its arms were so short that it could not reach the lemming that clung tenaciously to its neck, and none of the other greeps had any idea what had happened. They were gaping at their demented comrade in dull wonder, Little Fur forgotten.

Little Fur was as shocked by Lim's attack as they. By the time two of the puzzled greeps had solved their confusion by clubbing their comrade unconscious, their leader was already loping over to stand before the ivy.

Little Fur froze, knowing she had lost another chance.

Then, out of the sky plummeted a black streak of screeching fury, talons outstretched—Crow! He raked the filthy cheek of the leader, who howled in rage and flailed his club at the air. The black bird swerved and banked, evading the greep's reach, then pecked hard at its nest of hair with a wickedly sharp beak.

Little Fur did not hesitate this time. She sped across the yard, dodging the greeps, and leaped into the ivy. She could not see Lim anywhere. She was halfway up the ivy when one of the greeps grabbed her foot and dragged her to the ground. She rolled over and glimpsed Crow screaming and circling above, but he could not descend because two of the greeps were waving their staves. As the leader of the greeps reached for her, Little Fur cried out to Crow to get help.

A moment later, a huge hand cuffed her into blackness.

When Little Fur awoke, pain was clawing at her skull. Groaning, she opened her eyes to a blaze of blinding sunlight, and realized with horror that she must be lying out in the open for any human to see. Ignoring her pain, she struggled to sit up, raising a hand to shade her eyes. At the same time, she felt something stir beside her, and a dry tongue touched her hand.

"Ginger," she mumbled. She saw that she was

inside the round house and that it was not the gray cat beside her, but Nobody, her white pelt radiant as snow in the bands of sunlight streaming through the window.

"I feared they had killed you," Little Fur whispered. She sat up despite the pain in her head and moved closer to the vixen, but Nobody did not rise.

"I am broken," she said softly. "You must leave me and go."

"I will not leave you," Little Fur said, touching the vixen gently. She reached inside Nobody, feeling out the pain and the hurt places. Little Fur's own pain made it hard for her to concentrate, but she saw enough to know that it was bones that were broken, and not the complicated delicate parts.

"You must go," Nobody said again.

Little Fur lifted off her pouches and loosened their drawstrings so she could spread out their contents. She did not have her most potent medicines with her, but she took out the strongest

30

herbs and seeds for suppressing pain and began grinding them into a powder with a little stone pestle. "Why did the greeps put us in here?" she wondered aloud, to stop herself from thinking about the pain swelling in her head and creeping down her neck.

"Perhaps the greeps brought us in here to kill us out of the sight of any humans but the harling stopped them," said Nobody. "I felt the surging of its power driving them away when I awoke. But it will not be able to stop a horde of trolls."

"If the greeps were supposed to kill us, the trolls will not come," Little Fur said, offering a pinch of the ground powder to the vixen and wishing she still had her water gourd.

Nobody's white throat worked as she struggled to swallow the bitter powder, but soon the smell of pain coming from her faded to drowsy relief. Yet she fought sleep to say, "The trolls will come to see that we are truly dead. And even if they do not come, humans will."

Little Fur knew she was right, for even humans must have heard the growls of the greeps and the screeching of Crow. Yet she could not just leave Nobody lying here, badly hurt. She glanced toward the crack and only then noticed that the square of sunlight had shifted slightly, and now illuminated a small golden bump of fur.

"Lim!" she cried, and crawled over to the lemming. She rested her hands lightly upon his fur and closed her eyes, the better to concentrate on sending her mind into the small form. Again, the pain in her own head made it hard for her to see properly, and she could not find any bleeding or broken place. Yet something was weakening the lemming. Little Fur cupped his small head in her hands, and Lim's eyes squinted open.

"I disobeyed," he said. "I have shamed my clan."

"You saved my life," Little Fur told him gently. "Now be still, for I must try to see where you are hurt."

"I am not hurt," said Lim. "I am only tired."

"Do not sleep," Little Fur said, more sharply than she intended, for the warning came to her from her healing instincts as strongly as a command. She said, more softly, "You must stay awake so it is easier for me to look inside you." She closed her eyes and strove again to find the problem. She found a cut above one ear and a bruise on the back of Lim's head, but these wounds were not serious enough to weaken the pulse of his life.

Becoming desperate, Little Fur crawled back to the herbs and seeds she had spread out. Nothing was needed for pain, since Lim felt none. She lifted a wax-stoppered nut gourd. In it was a tiny ball of stuff that would slow all the workings of life in the one who nibbled it. After a moment, she set it down again, because the substance would almost certainly make Lim sleep.

Nobody watched as Little Fur lifted up another gourd and unstoppered it. A strong, sharp sweetness filled the air, and she hesitated only a moment before crawling back to Lim with the gourd and dribbling a little of the dark liquid between his teeth. "This will strengthen you," she said.

"I am so tired," Lim said softly. But the liquid roused him slightly, and this time Little Fur found something under the cut at his temple. It was not a wound, but some shadowy part of the lemming that did not feel right. Little Fur could not make her senses delicate enough to enter the darkness so that she could understand it, but she was certain it was this that was sapping Lim's life.

"Healer, you must leave this place," Nobody said urgently.

"Even if I could leave you, I cannot leave Lim," Little Fur replied.

"Then take him with you," the vixen said. "He is small enough for you to carry. Do not trouble yourself about me. The humans will simply put me in a cage, and maybe summon a healer to tend to me."

Strange as this sounded, Little Fur knew Nobody was right, for despite their violent destructiveness, humans could sometimes show great tenderness toward beasts. And while she hated the idea of Nobody being caged, at least she would be alive and might be rescued. Little Fur got to her feet and went unsteadily to the door, but it would not budge. She sniffed and only then understood that the door was barred.

They were trapped!

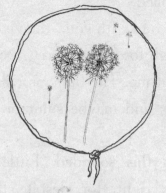

CHAPTER 3
The Severing

Lim gave a soft moan, and Little Fur went to kneel beside him. She was glad to have something to distract her from their plight. But her spirits plummeted at once, for although the lemming's eyes were open, they had lost their shining brightness. She leaned over him and called his name, but Lim seemed unable to see her.

Frightened, Little Fur again put her hands around his head and closed her eyes. She bent all her will on the shadowy place under the bruise, but her mind felt clumsy. She could not make it small enough to get inside and heal whatever was wrong. For the first time in her life, she felt utterly helpless.

I must concentrate, she told herself fiercely. *I must forget the pain in my head, the locked door and the fact that trolls or humans might come at any moment. I must think only of Lim.*

"Teta . . . ," the lemming moaned softly.

Little Fur sent her mind deeper into him, seeking his spirit. She felt it struggling against an immense weariness that flowed from the shadowy place. Lim was like a little beast caught in a swift-flowing stream. She tried to pour strength into him, but it seemed to her that the sinister shadow in his mind was growing. *I will sing to make his spirit stronger,* she told herself, but before she could begin, the lemming's eyelids fluttered open.

"I have to sleep," he murmured. Then his eyes closed and the pulse of his life winked out.

Little Fur stared down at him, shocked. She looked at her hands and saw that they were trembling. She reached for Lim's small body, but could not bring herself to touch him and feel the warmth of life fading away.

It was a long time before she heard Nobody calling her through the roaring confusion in her mind. Lacking the will to stand, she crawled to the vixen. Her eyes fell on the healing pouches. All at once, her carefully chosen selection of seeds and herbs and her little gourds of potions seemed no more than a muddle of leaves and sticks and seeds blown together by the wind.

"Little Fur, hear me!" Nobody urged. "I can smell a human coming."

"The door is locked," Little Fur said dully.

"I know," Nobody said. "But the human will open it. You must hide!"

"I can't leave Lim," she murmured.

"You cannot help him anymore!" the injured vixen insisted. "Hide yourself or the human will catch you!"

The urgency in her voice drove Little Fur to obey. She groped her way to the fissure and half tumbled into it. Then she drew the elf cloak over her head and waited to see what the human would do.

There was a rattling sound; then the door opened and something filled the sunlit opening: a bulky human-shaped darkness with light streaming all around it. It stood in the doorway for a long time. Little Fur could smell that it was trying to see into the shadowy round house with its weak eyes. At length it uttered a grunt of surprise and stooped to enter. Little Fur held her breath as light flooded in, revealing the bodies of Lim and the white fox. The human went first to Lim's body. It bent down and touched the lemming gently. Then it picked Lim up, muttering words that smelled of pity and puzzlement, stroking the soft fur. Finally it straightened and glanced around.

Nobody gave a low whine to draw the human's attention. It began at once to give off the stink of fear. Nobody gave another soft moan, and the human's fear gave way to the scent of compassion and kindly concern. The human gently laid

Lim's body in a bag it carried over its shoulder and moved cautiously toward the fox. It knelt close beside her and held out its hand, palm down. It gave off a smell of anxiety, but Nobody did not bite. Very slowly and carefully, the human slid its big hands under her. The vixen whined in pain, but still she did not bite. As the human straightened, holding her, Little Fur smelled that Nobody had fainted.

The human carried Nobody out of the round house, stooping again to pass through the low door. Little Fur climbed out and crept through the door. The dew-spangled grass sparkled in the blaze of sunlight, but Little Fur did not take her eyes away from the human. It had reached the base of one of the high houses, and even as she watched, it passed through a door and out of sight, carrying Nobody.

Little Fur took a deep breath and hurried across to the ivy-clad wall. She felt as if a thousand humans were watching her from the high houses. But she did not falter, because she knew that her father's elf cloak would prevent any human from seeing her and she must get help for Nobody. If only she had not been so quick to send Crow away! And where had he got to? Surely time enough had passed for him to have found Sorrow. She knew Ginger would be harder to find, because he was away from the wilderness seeking the one-eyed cat Sly.

Little Fur scaled the ivy-covered wall, her hands and feet as clumsy as if she had borrowed them. At last she stood in the cobbled lane on the other side of the wall. She shuddered anew at the memory of how easily Lim had died under her hands. She shook her head and told herself that she must find somewhere to hide until night. The trouble was that her mind seemed not to be working properly. She kept seeing Lim attacking the greep, or Nobody being carried away into a high house by the human. She felt overwhelmed by a despair so strong that it numbed her.

"There is something wrong with me," Little Fur muttered.

Then a dreadful thought came to her.

Heart thundering, Little Fur turned and thrust her hands into the tangle of ivy hanging from the stone wall. Earth magic was flowing through it—she had felt it before the greep had seized her—but now she could feel nothing. She had a vision of the greep picking her up roughly at the behest of the harling and carrying her to the stone house, unwittingly severing her from the flow of earth magic. Maybe the greeps had been ordered to sever her from the flow of magic. The Troll King might have guessed that this would be the cruelest blow.

Tears blurred Little Fur's eyes, and she sank down and wept.

She had been severed from the flow of earth magic! No wonder she had not been able to save Lim! If only she had been more wary! If only she had refused the pleading of the mink!

The sound of human voices in the distance reminded her of where she was, and she got to her feet, knowing she must find a place to hide until it was safe for her to make her way home. But she could not go home. The Old Ones would never allow one who was not open to the flow of earth magic to enter the secret wilderness.

Little Fur stumbled to an open cellar window in one of the human dwellings lining a cobbled lane. There was no need to search for a shelter with an earthen floor now. The cellar was damp and smelled unpleasantly of old human rubbish, but Little Fur did not care. She climbed down into it, wrapped herself in her father's cloak, and escaped into sleep.

Little Fur dreamed that she was hurrying along a tunnel leading down to the troll city of Underth. Inscribed on the walls were strange, beautiful runes that had been made by trolls, and even though she knew she ought to be hurrying, she could not resist stopping to study them. She felt that if she stared at them long enough, she would know what they meant.

When did the trolls make these? she wondered. No one answered, but she sensed someone was watching her. The feeling was so strong that she awoke and opened her eyes.

A glowing green eye was looking at her. She gasped and shrank back, only to realize that she knew the scent of its owner. "Sly?" she whispered, her eyes picking out the black shape of the cat within the dense shadow of the cellar.

"I thought it was you, Healer, but you do not smell like yourself," said the black cat.

"You were looking for me?"

"Crow saw me when he was flying to the wilderness to tell Sorrow and Ginger what happened," Sly said, her green eye narrowing. "He said greeps had caught you and were going to eat you."

"I do not think they meant to eat me," Little

Fur said. She told Sly quickly about the harling, Lim's death, and Nobody's being taken away by a human.

"How did you escape?" asked Sly.

"I hid when the human came, and when it carried Nobody out of the round house, I slipped out, too."

"That was clever," the black cat said approvingly. "Do not worry about the vixen. The humans will not hurt her. They like things that are different."

"They will put her in a cage," Little Fur said.

Sly's eye glinted. "Humans are very fond of caging wild things, but cages can be opened."

"Yes," Little Fur said, heartened by the cat's cool certainty. Then a thought struck her. "Did you free Danger from the zoo?" She knew the black cat had done nothing since meeting the caged panther but plot to free him.

"I will free him this very night," Sly said exultantly. "Indeed, I must go now. You had better return to the wilderness."

"Oh, Sly, I *can't*," Little Fur said. "I can never go there again, because the greeps severed me from the flow of earth magic. I can't even heal properly now. That is why Lim died."

"You must find the way to undo this severing," Sly said.

In that moment, a solution came to Little Fur like a beam of sunlight slicing through a winter sky. "I will ask the Sett Owl how I can rejoin the flow!" she said.

Sly gave a scornful hiss. "Ginger said that I should ask the Sett Owl how to rescue Danger. I went and I asked, but the bird told me that his freedom was not mine to give, and that all was not as it seemed. She said that Danger must follow the fearful guide in order to find himself."

"What does that mean?" Little Fur asked.

"It means nothing," Sly said coldly, springing up onto the sill of the cellar window.

Even as the black cat vanished, Little Fur suddenly remembered what she had wanted to tell her. "Sly! Don't forget that Danger said he would kill you if you let him out!" she called, but the cat had already gone.

Little Fur climbed out the cellar window into the lane. It was deep night, and the moon was hidden behind a thick bank of cloud. It was very dark, despite the false light shining from a pole. The lane looked very different at night, but instead of noting the differences, Little Fur could only feel the terrible silence of the mossy earth between the cobbles. She set a course for the Sett Owl's beaked house, thinking, *This is how it is for humans. No wonder they feel nothing for the earth or the earth spirit. Perhaps they build their roads to block out the deadness of the land.*

Little Fur had just reached the hedge beside the beaked

47

house when Ginger and Sorrow found her. The red fox had grown strong and his coat sleek and thick since his return from Underth, but there was still a deep sadness in his eyes. Thinking of all the trials he had endured made Little Fur ashamed of the selfishness of her grief. After all, she was not the first nor would she be the last creature in the world to suffer.

"Crow spoke true," Ginger said in his low, purring voice. "Earth magic does not flow through you."

Little Fur nodded. "I am going to ask the Sett Owl if there is a way for me to repair the severing."

Sorrow looked troubled. "The Sett Owl is very old. It is as if the world grows ever more complex in her eyes, and while Indyk is very skillful at explaining her words, I dinna ken if his words count as foretellings."

Little Fur repeated her story again. When she came to the part where the human had carried Nobody away, Sorrow's eyes blazed yellow with outrage. "She must not be caged!" he said, growling deep in his throat.

"I do not think the human that carried her away meant to hurt her," Little Fur said, but the fox seemed not to hear her. He began pacing feverishly. Watching him, Little Fur felt a sudden lightening at the thought that  rescuing the white vixen might open the shell in which the fox had encased his heart.

"You ought to go and see if you can find where the human took her," she urged. "Did Crow tell you where it all happened?"

"He did," said Sorrow. He held her gaze for a moment, taut with indecision, and then something in him gave way, and he bounded off.

Little Fur and Ginger exchanged a look; then they crawled under the hedge. Clambering to her feet on the other side, Little Fur dimly saw the crossed sticks set at the tip of the steep roof that had given the beaked house its name. Little Fur took a deep breath and told herself that the Sett Owl had offered her good advice in the past.

"Have courage," Ginger whispered, pressing his soft forehead against hers. "I will wait here for you."

Little Fur took a deep breath and tucked up her tunic. Then, gathering the shreds of her courage, she crawled into the tunnel at the base of the wall.

CHAPTER 4
The Sett Owl

Inside the beaked house, a dim jeweled light streaked the floor, the rows of wooden benches, the pallid marble statues of giant humans, and the somber gray walls. There was no sign of the Sett Owl, nor were there any of the beasts who were usually waiting their turn to make their offerings and present their questions.

As soon as Little Fur climbed out of the tunnel that ran under the wall, she felt the fizzing of still magic in the air. She took comfort from the fact that it pressed against her skin and nuzzled at her as fondly as it had always done. She had once believed that the beaked house had given the Sett Owl the power to see the future, and had lengthened her life. Now she knew that the owl had already had the seeds of her power when she had taken refuge in the beaked house. The still magic had simply recognized and nourished what was in her.

The humans had no idea of the existence of still magic, though it had grown from the songs and yearnings that they had brought into the beaked house. Little Fur did not know why, but the magic had an affectionate regard for her that seemed to be unchanged, despite her being severed from the flow of earth magic. She had always thought it liked the earth magic that flowed through her, but now she saw that this could not be so. It was odd to imagine that it might simply like her, as one creature likes another. Suddenly Little Fur realized that the faint smell that had so mystified her in the round house was exactly this—the scent of still magic!

"Greetings, Little Fur," said a familiar voice. "I have been expecting you." The small monkey Indyk emerged from the shadows behind one of the great stone forms.

"The Sett Owl foresaw my coming?" Little Fur asked.

"She did," Indyk said gravely.

"Where is Gem?" Little Fur asked.

"In a small wooden house at the end of the yard," said the monkey. "She fears to enter the beaked house. She fears the still magic."

"*Fears* it?" Little Fur echoed.

"Unfortunately, yes," said the monkey, sounding tired. "You have come to seek a foretelling, Healer?"

Little Fur nodded, then realized that she had forgotten that she would need to bring an offering. "I have a question, but I have no offering," she said apologetically. She meant to add that she would go and find something, but the monkey gave her a long measuring look before saying that he would summon the Sett Owl.

After he had vanished back into the shadows, Little Fur studied the giant stone humans, wondering as she always did at the compassion in their expressions. Humans had made them look that way, but now Little Fur felt as if the enormous stone humans were gazing down at her with pity, understanding her loss.

The flutter of wings interrupted Little Fur's thoughts. She looked up to see the Sett Owl descending on ragged outstretched wings through a swirl of dust motes. She landed awkwardly, and Little Fur was shocked to see how frail she had become, and how cloudy her enormous eyes were.

"Greetings, Sett Owl," Little Fur whispered.

The Sett Owl clacked her beak and said in a rasping voice, "Greetings, Healer. You have no offering, but I will accept your question if you will grant me a boon."

Little Fur nodded, and said quietly, "I am severed from the flow of earth magic."

"Yes," agreed the Sett Owl.

"Can it be undone?" Little Fur asked.

"All is not as it seems," said the Sett Owl.

Around Little Fur, the still magic pressed against her like hands seeking something hidden. "The she-wizard foresaw what will come, and you must not fail her vision. You must go to the source in order to understand what you must do."

Little Fur was puzzled at the mention of a she-wizard. Surely this foretelling was similar to the one that Sly had received. Perhaps the Sett Owl was confused. "Sett Owl, it is I, Little Fur," she began.

"The beloved," said the Sett Owl dreamily.

Little Fur blinked in surprise. "I do not understand," she said.

"No," agreed the Sett Owl. "To understand how you came to be as you are is the nature of the quest you must now undertake."

"But I know what happened," Little Fur said hastily. "The Troll King sent some greeps to sever me from the flow of earth magic, or maybe it was simply an accident."

"The Troll King sent the greeps to steal the green stone you wear," said the owl. Little Fur felt for the stone left to her by her mother, but it was safe around her neck. The Sett Owl continued, "The Troll King believes the stone is not empty, but he is wrong: only with understanding can the stone be refilled, and that which is sundered be healed. Only at the source will there be understanding, but the way is perilous."

"What source? What way?" Little Fur asked desperately, because she could see the Sett Owl's eyelids beginning to droop.

The owl opened her eyes wide and the clouds in them drew aside, leaving a clear round whirl of stars and constellations. "I have no more answers to give, Healer," the Sett Owl said. "I have answered the one who comes without an offering to ask the last and the first question. I am no longer the Sett Owl." Her eyes closed.

Little Fur had a wild desire to shake the old bird. The violence of the impulse shocked her, and she stepped back in dismay. Was this rage of emptiness and confusion what humans felt? And trolls? No wonder they did so much harm!

"Healer?" Indyk proffered a bowl of water. "You smell of thirst."

Little Fur wanted to slap the water away, but she forced herself to take the bowl and drink a few sips, resolving to keep control of the impatience that had taken root in her heart.

"I did not understand the foretelling," she told the monkey as she gave the bowl back to him. "And surely the Sett Owl said some of the same words to Sly."

"Some readings are so large that they touch upon many lives," Indyk told her gravely, setting the bowl aside.

"But how can Sly's wanting to free Danger have anything to do with me?"

"Perhaps the similarity was only seeming, and there is no connection. Yet the Sett Owl sees links that others do not," Indyk said. "And remember that the words of the deepest foretellings are riddles that want solving."

"A *riddle*," Little Fur echoed. The word tasted

tricky and complicated on her tongue and in her mind.

"Only in understanding the riddle can its solution be found."

Again Little Fur felt a surge of anger, but she choked it back to ask, "Why couldn't she just tell me what to do?"

"I am surprised you would ask that," Indyk said softly.

Little Fur's anger ebbed before the gentle dignity of the monkey's response. She looked again at the frail owl and felt a pity so strong that it hurt her, for what had all her power done but use her up? She thought of the last words said to her by the owl and asked softly, "What did she mean by saying that she was no longer the Sett Owl?"

"Herness told me, when first I came here to the beaked house to stay, that one day a creature would come without an offering to ask a question that would be the largest she had ever been asked, and answering it would quench her."

Little Fur was aghast. "My question—"

"For which you owe a boon," Indyk said, and there was sadness in his eyes. "You must ask the first question."

"The first?" Little Fur repeated dully, but the monkey had turned to tenderly groom the sleeping owl.

After a moment, she went quietly to the tunnel entrance and crawled back outside, devastated to think that her question had used up the last of the Sett Owl's power. And what on earth was the meaning of the boon she had been asked for? What was the first question, and of whom ought she to ask it?

Little Fur strove to calm herself by concentrating on the things she *had* understood. The Sett Owl said that the Troll King had never meant to kill her or sever her from the flow of earth magic. He had only intended the greeps to steal the green stone. The harling had obviously prevented the theft. But what did the Troll King want with her stone when he had his own? The Sett Owl said he believed the stone was full, but how could a stone be full of anything but itself? Little Fur had been given more questions than answers.

The most puzzling part of the telling was the mention of a she-wizard, for there were no wizards in this age, any more than there were full-blooded elves. The only wizard Little Fur knew anything about was the she-wizard of the last age, who had captured her mother, a troll princess, and her father, an elf warrior. The wizard had kept them imprisoned until the hatred between the elf and the troll faded and they became allies. Their attempts to escape failed, but in time friendship turned to love, and Little Fur had been conceived. Only then had the wizard told them that the child they had made was the reason she had held them captive. During the flood that ended the age of magic, Little Fur's father had cracked open the earth and sacrificed his life to save his troll princess and the baby she carried.

But the Sett Owl had seemed to be saying something quite different. *The she-wizard foresaw what will come, and you must not fail her vision.* It was almost as if she had contrived for Little Fur to be born so that she could do something in *this* age of the world.

"Healer?" said Ginger when Little Fur emerged from the end of the tunnel into the moonlight.

Little Fur looked into the gray cat's orange eyes. "She said I must go to the source, but I do not know what source she meant."

"What else could she mean but the source of the flow of earth magic?" said Ginger simply.

Little Fur stared into his bright eyes and wondered if dull-wittedness was another effect of being severed from the flow of earth magic.

"The source of earth magic is the earth spirit itself," Ginger continued. "Did the Sett Owl say how you are to find it?"

Little Fur shook her head. "She said only that the way was perilous." She noticed a small horde of lemmings clustered nearby, talking quietly, and remembered urging the Teta to send some of her people to ask the advice of the Sett Owl.

How long ago that seemed to Little Fur, though it was only the day before!

"Greetings, Healer," said one of the lemmings courteously.

"Greetings," Little Fur said. "I have to tell you that Lim has—"

"He has joined the world's dream," said the lemming with such serenity that Little Fur was shocked, not because the lemmings had known before she told them—for many animals had a clan link that told them of the death of one of their number—but because of their calmness in the face of that death.

Perhaps it is part of their creed of politeness to greet death with this gentle acceptance, Little Fur thought. *And why not, for do not all creatures die eventually?* Maybe if she herself had not been severed from the flow of earth magic, she would not have felt such raw sorrow at Lim's death. But without earth magic to connect her to all other living things, a death was a terrible severing. Little Fur forced herself to describe Lim's bravery to the listening lemmings.

"Thank you," said one of the lemmings gravely. "We will send a messenger to the clan to tell of his courage, but we wait now to consult the Sett Owl."

"She . . . she will answer no more questions," stammered Little Fur.

"We do not mean the *old* Sett Owl," said a lemming placidly. "We spoke to her yesterday. She said that we must wait to ask our question of the *new* Sett Owl. She said that today would be the day the new Sett Owl will answer her first question."

Little Fur pressed her hands to her face, suddenly understanding the boon asked by the Sett Owl. She was to ask the first question of Gem, who feared the beaked house and the still magic. She was to be the means of forcing Gem to become the Sett Owl, despite knowing that the calling would devour the little owl's life, just as it had done to the old owl. Little Fur felt sick. Of course, Gem could refuse the request, but she would not refuse Little Fur, who had cared for her ever since the Sett Owl had insisted that the owlet was her responsibility.

The lemmings watched her with their small bright eyes full of earnest courtesy. It was all Little Fur could do to ask them where she could find Gem. Several of them pointed to a rough timber hut at the end of the cobbled yard, and Little Fur turned and went slowly toward it. As she neared it, the grizzled rat Gazrak came scuttling out, baring his yellow fangs.

"Stop!" he snarled. "It is sacrilegion for anyone to coming here without being per-missioned." Then the furious red light in the big rat's eyes faded to wary pink as he recognized Little Fur.

"Greetings, Healer," he said sullenly, plucking uncomfortably with one claw at the grass and leaves with which he had decorated himself.

"Greetings, Protector of the Small Herness," Little Fur said, marveling that she could sound so calm when a storm of uncertainties raged inside her. "I must speak to Gem."

Gem's self-appointed guardian narrowed his eyes suspiciously. "What is Little Fur wanting of Small Herness?"

"I will tell that to her," Little Fur said.

Gazrak gave a long hiss of frustration. "Small Herness not being here! Now that she can fly, she must soar and hunt! I told her that a Sett Owl has more important things to do. But she says she cannot be Sett Owl, and she will not!" He twitched his ragged ears in a mixture of anxiety and ire. "Stupid Crow should never have shown her how to fly! She flew up, and now her head is full of clouds!" This was said with real venom, and Little Fur guessed the rat was jealous of Gem's fondness for Crow.

"I am sure she will return soon," Little Fur said.

Gazrak all but spat at her in his fury, "You

66

know nothing, Healer! Herness will never escape the clouds in her head!"

Suddenly there was a flutter of wings overhead, and a moment later Gem landed, hooting softly with laughter.  To Little Fur's surprise, Crow landed beside her a few wingbeats later.

Ignoring the sleek black bird, Gazrak rushed up to the small owl and began grooming her anxiously, smoothing feathers that were untidy because she had not lost all of her baby down. Gem bore the rat's attention stoically, letting him fuss until he had calmed himself down.

"Herness must be careful," Gazrak scolded at last.

"Dear Protector," Gem said, and she reached out and pecked tenderly at Gazrak's scarred head.

Gazrak seemed almost transfixed, but then he shook himself and told Gem with much haughtiness that Little Fur wished to consult with her.

"Thank you, Protector," Gem said meekly. This seemed to mollify the rat, who went scuttling away with his nose in the air.

"Stupidness," Crow snorted.

"He is my protector, and you are my brother," Gem said reproachfully. "I love you both and wish you would not always fight. It makes my head hurt."

Crow ruffled his feathers and looked slightly ashamed.

"Greetings, Gem," Little Fur said, kneeling down beside Gem. The owlet immediately fluttered up onto her shoulder and tried to snuggle into Little Fur's wild red hair, just as she had done when they had traveled together to the ice mountains. But Gem had grown, and after a moment, she fluttered from Little Fur's shoulder to perch upon a metal post rising from the earth.

"Bigness is not a thing that can be avoided," Gem observed wistfully.

CHAPTER 5
The Guide

"I have been to see the Sett Owl," Little Fur said slowly.

"The Sett Owl is the perfection of bigness," Gem said. "There is no other like her."

"I think it is true that there will never be another like her," Little Fur agreed.

Gem said nothing, but the laughter was fading from her round, gold-flecked eyes.

Little Fur tried to think of what was fair to say and what was true. Finally, she said baldly, "I told the Sett Owl that I had been severed from the flow of earth magic. I asked if there was a way for the severing to be undone." Then she repeated as exactly as she could all the words that the Sett Owl had said.

"A boon?" Crow croaked, shifting his plumage uneasily. "What boon?"

But Little Fur was gazing at Gem. She said, "Do you know where I can find the earth spirit, if that is what the Sett Owl meant by 'the source'? Do you know how a stone can be full or empty, or why the Sett Owl spoke of a she-wizard?"

Crow gave a rude caw of disgust. "Stupidness! How can stone being full of anything but its own self? And what is Little Fur having to doing with wizards? Wizard-folk nevermore walking and casting in the worldliness."

"Wizards were farsighted, it is said," Gem murmured without meeting Little Fur's gaze. "A wizard might see from one age to the next."

"Perhaps the wizard who forced my parents to love one another was not evil," Little Fur said softly.

"Perhaps a thing may look evil, though it is not," Gem conceded. She fluffed her feathers and added, almost defiantly, "I must sleep now. I am weary from hunting."

You are afraid, thought Little Fur. The words in her mind were sharp as a beak seeking a soft place to peck, but she did not speak them, for who would not fear to face the fate of the Sett Owl, if they were wise?

As if Little Fur had spoken aloud, Gem made a little whirring noise in her throat. Then she said forlornly, "If I go into the beaked house, I will grow, but I will never soar again." Little Fur longed to gather the tiny owl up and tell her that she need not enter the beaked house and become the Sett Owl, that she might soar and hunt and be with her own kind. Except that Gem had never spent time with other owls. As a fallen nestling, she had been shunned, and the Sett Owl had told Little Fur that

71

a fallen owl could never be as other owls. That Gem must fly up to what she might be.

Fly UP, thought Little Fur. "Perhaps there are many ways to soar," she murmured. "Perhaps the Sett Owl soared where no other could fly, because of the still magic." Then she reached out to stroke Gem's soft wings, first one and then the other, adding gently, "But, Gem dear, in the end it is you who must decide what to do."

"If I do not go into the beaked house, you will never feel the earth spirit again," Gem said. "And I have seen that each day that you are severed from it, your elf blood will wither a little more until there is no elf blood left in you. But if I go into the beaked house, I have seen that I will send you into dreadful danger."

Little Fur stared at her, aghast. "Did you see that just now when you looked at me?"

"I saw these things the last time I went inside the beaked house. I saw so much, and yet I could not see the end of anything. It made me fear what harm I might do."

Little Fur said softly, "No matter what you see and what you tell me, Gem, in the end it is I who must decide what to do. You are not to blame for what I decide, or for what comes of my decision."

There was a long silence. Little Fur could smell Gem's fear and wondered if the owl was too young to have to make the choice. Perhaps, instead of growing when the still magic filled her up, she would crack like an egg. This thought was so strong that Little Fur realized it was one of Gem's fears.

Then something happened.

Little Fur felt a great silent cry shiver the air. Her hair crackled with the force of it, and the tips of her ears tingled. There was a great rustling commotion. All of the pigeons and owls and other birds that roosted in the walls of the beaked house rose up as one and began to weave a vast, complex net in the air above the beaked house. On the ground, Ginger, Gazrak, and the lemmings were gazing up at the birds.

"The Sett Owl has joined the world's dream,"

Crow said solemnly, and he rose up to join the net of birds.

"I did not say goodbye to her," Little Fur said. Her eyes filled with hot tears, and she pressed her hand to the pain in her chest. She felt again the same ache that she had felt when the bright pulse of Lim's life had been snuffed out. She understood then, as she had never been able to before, that this was why humans feared death: because for them, as for all creatures that held themselves separate from other creatures, death was the bitterest and most final of endings.

Little Fur gazed up for a long time at the hundreds and hundreds of birds wheeling in the sky overhead. Only when her neck grew sore did she look down and see that Gem had not moved. The tiny owl was still sitting atop the metal post. Her eyes were closed, but she was not sleeping. All of her plumage was fluffed out, and she was shivering so hard that her tiny beak rattled.

"What is it?" Little Fur asked anxiously.

"Afraid," whispered Gem.

"Do not be afraid," Little Fur said. "No one will make you go into the beaked house."

"Not me," Gem said, her eyes opening.

"The Sett Owl?" Little Fur asked confusedly. "You need not fear for her."

"I do not fear for her," Gem said. "She has joined the world's dream."

"Then what do you fear?"

"It is not me that fears. It is the still magic," Gem said, and now her enormous eyes were fixed on the beaked house. "It . . . it loved the Sett Owl, and now she has gone away. It is afraid. . . . It is *calling*."

Little Fur stared at her in astonishment. "I hear nothing."

"That is because it is not calling you," Gem whispered. She launched herself into the air on soundless wings and flew like an arrow to the small opening above the great doors that humans used to enter the beaked house. When she disappeared through it, Gazrak gave a squeal of dismay and raced across the grass to vanish through the tunnel at the base of the wall.

Little Fur sped after them, stunned that so much had happened so quickly. She crawled through the tunnel after Gazrak, but it was not until she reentered the beaked house that she felt the roaring confusion of the still magic. It was like a silent storm that battered against stone and cobbles and wood. Yet all was utterly quiet. There was no sign of Indyk, but Gem was perched atop the carved back of a throne such as elf kings and queens had sat upon in the last age. Light rained down on her through one of the colored windows. Her eyes were closed. Gazrak stood below her, gazing up and wringing his paws.

Little Fur did not dare to speak, but as she stood there, she felt that the wild churning of the still magic had begun to fall into a pattern. The pattern was coming from Gem, who was making a soft, rhythmic thrumming sound. The thrumming slowed and the pattern slowed until at last the still magic was still again. For a moment, Little Fur felt the same depthless peace she always felt when surrounded by a power so great, a power that simply existed without doing anything.

Then Gem's eyes opened, and the golden flecks in them moved and shimmered like stars.

"I am sorry," Little Fur said.

"No," Gem said. It was her voice, but there was no longer fear in it, or wistfulness, and behind it shimmered all the power and mystery of the still magic. "You granted your boon to the one who was before me. You asked a question, but then you told me that I did not need to answer it. You made my fear be quiet so that I could hear the still magic calling me. Now you will have an answer."

Little Fur's heart bumped in her throat. "My answer?"

"To the question I did not answer," Gem said calmly. "You asked where the earth spirit was to be found. This cannot be told, but there is one who can guide you, though that one is mad, and danger will travel with you as well."

"Who will guide me?" Little Fur asked.

"He," said Gem. Her eyes shifted to the tunnel opening. A gray-furred creature with startling tufts of fur at the tips of his ears was emerging from it. He was not much bigger than Ginger, and his movements were uncertain and timid. When he looked at her, Little Fur saw that he had eyes as red as wildfire, and when he straightened and turned to look around, she saw his long, beautiful tail, dramatically banded in black and white. It was the tail that reminded Little Fur that she had seen creatures like this one before in the human zoo! Lemuri, they called themselves.

She looked back to Gem and said doubtfully, "This lemur will guide me to the earth spirit?"

"None knows the way," answered Gem. "The lemur will dream the way."

The lemur crept closer to Gem, and Little Fur saw how madness burned in his eyes. "You are the one I dreamed: the Sett Owl," he said. "But I could not find you."

"I was not made until just now," said Gem.

"Will you stop my dreams?" begged the lemur hoarsely.

"I cannot," said Gem. "You must follow them until they cease. But you will not follow them alone. One already follows your dreams, and here is another who will go with you. Still others there are that will follow your dreams until they discover their own."

The lemur shuddered violently from head to toe and then caught up his tail in his paws and began to gnaw the tip distractedly. Seeing this, Little Fur remembered the bedraggled lemur from the zoo. He had uttered gibberish while another of his clan had pronounced him mad. But the same lemur had also said that sometimes Ofred dreamed true.

"You are Ofred," said Little Fur. "How did you get out of the zoo?"

"A cat freed me because she needed my hands

to turn a key," replied the lemur. Some of the things this small creature had said to h e rat the zoo floated back into Little Fur's mind. He had warned that she would lose her way and that she would be devoured by darkness if she did not find the deepest green.

The lemur gave a wild shriek of laughter, and the sound made the hair on Little Fur's toes bristle. "Ofred remembers you," the lemur said, his eyes blazing with accusation. "Little Fur, the elf troll whose face is in the flow of earth magic! In nightmare has Ofred seen you!"

"Nightmare?" Little Fur asked.

Ofred sang, in a sweet but mournful voice, "The way is deep and dark and doomed, and all who take it must be consumed!" The last word was a sob, and then the lemur shuddered. He lifted his tail around his shoulders before burying his small muzzle in it.

Little Fur looked helplessly at Gem, wondering how this tormented animal could lead her to the earth spirit. But Gem was looking at the tunnel opening again. The lemmings were entering, soft-footed and diffident. They came and laid down several soft white tulip bulbs before the small owl, and then, as one, they pressed themselves to the ground as a sign of deep respect.

"Greetings, Sett Owl," said a lemming. "We bring an offering and ask if you can tell us the meaning of the nightmares of the Teta."

"The nightmares come because the clan grows too big," said Gem. "The clan must divide, and some must go far away. If it does not, madness will come and the clan will fail."

"Will those who go find safe territory?" asked another lemming, showing no sign of alarm or fear.

"Those that would go must follow the dreams of Ofred," said Gem, nodding at the lemur. "Those that dare to follow him to the end will find a strange but wondrous territory."

The lemmings glanced uncertainly and uneasily at one another.

"Lemmings do not seek strangeness," said a different lemming, very respectfully.

The lemmings pressed themselves to the ground again and departed as quietly as they had entered. Gazrak hurried to gather up their offering, his eyes shining with greed.

Little Fur looked back at Gem, and again an angry impatience stirred in her. "It is all very well to follow Ofred's dreams, but they seem not to tell us where we are to go or when."

"The lemur will dream," Gem said serenely. "Take care, Little Fur, for while you are cut off from the flow of earth magic, your elf blood weakens and your troll blood strengthens and grows unruly. Do not let it master you."

Little Fur felt as if she had been drenched in icy water. "What will happen if it does?"

"You will never again feel the flow of earth magic, for trollkind has closed itself so utterly to the flow that no troll could ever rejoin it," said the small owl who had been Gem and who was now wholly the Sett Owl of the beaked house.

"There is no safeness in having a mad lemur as guide," Crow said later that night. "Madness equals stupidness and dangerousness."

"I do not think there is any use in thinking of safety," Little Fur said in a low voice.

Crow gave a low Craaak! and tried to look grave, but he was falling asleep.

Little Fur sighed and glanced at the enormous tree in whose branches the lemur now slept. *Is he dreaming yet?* she wondered uneasily. She went to sit on a stone step below a lesser door to the beaked house. The moon had set, and stars were beginning to wink out one by one. It would not be long before it was time for the sun to open its eye, and then the human guardians who tended the beaked house would arrive.

Little Fur stood and then sat again, restless.

She had never felt this itching of the spirit so strongly before. She knew it must signal the strengthening of her troll blood. Gem's warning that she must be careful had frightened her. Never had she thought of her troll blood as bad or dangerous, but it seemed this was only because it had been balanced by her elf blood. Yet if pure troll blood was dark and unruly, did that mean her mother had been bad? And if so, how had her father come to love her mother?

These questions made her head ache, so she turned her thoughts to the lemmings. Those who had spoken to Gem had departed immediately after their audience. Two hours later, the lemmings who wanted to make the exodus had begun arriving in small groups. By the time Ofred had settled to dream, there were hundreds of lemmings sleeping at the foot of the tree. They slept so close together that they looked like a great misshapen creature with a mottled coat.

Little Fur tried to imagine how it would be to travel with such a horde, all of them led by a mad lemur. She could not see it. Yet Gem had said there was no other way.

Little Fur stood up again and paced, wishing that Ginger would return with the fresh healing pouches he had promised to fetch so that she could talk over everything with him. She was also worried about Sly. Clearly there had been a link between their quests, for she was sure it was Sly who had freed the lemur. She had wanted to know more about Sly and what had happened at the zoo, but Ofred had only whimpered when she had asked him. Little Fur went back to the step and sat again, rubbing her eyes and wondering if Sorrow had found Nobody yet.

Suddenly there was a rustling of leaves and Ofred dropped lightly to a lower branch. Little Fur rose to her feet and waited.

CHAPTER 6
Danger

For a moment, Ofred seemed not to see Little Fur, but then he looked at her and pointed to the horizon. "I dreamed of the place where the land meets the great sea," he said.

Little Fur stared at him in dismay. "We are to go to the great sea?" she asked, unbelieving. Her friend Brownie the pony had told her that earth magic did not flow through the salten sea as it did through fresh water.

The lemur made no response. He was gazing

about in a startled, fearful way, as if he had heard someone calling his name from different places all at once. He did not notice the lemmings, most of whom still slept soundly about him. He pointed again, but in a completely different direction, and said, "The great sea waits for us with a gifting and a maw that will swallow us." Then he put one of his paws in his mouth and began to suck it.

Little Fur sighed. So this was to be the way of it. The lemur would tell them his dreams, and *she* would have to figure out how to understand them. And it was not only herself that she would be deciding for, but the lemmings, too. She looked crossly at them and then was ashamed, for had she not failed Lim after he had saved her life? Was not something owed for that?

Little Fur straightened her shoulders and drew her cloak about her, trying to recall all she knew of the great sea. It was quite a lot, thanks to Brownie, who was taken by his human to the seaside each winter. She remembered that he had said that there was a river that flowed to the salten sea. Surely, then, they only had to find the right river and follow it.

When Crow awoke, Little Fur told him her plan.

"Crow knowing way to river to the great sea!" the black bird said eagerly. "Crow can leading the way."

This seemed a good omen and helped Little Fur keep her temper as she roused the lemmings, who each needed to be shaken gently several times before they were properly awake. Crow said they might be able to reach the edge of the city before the sun opened its eye if they moved fast. Little Fur did not know where they could hide the horde of lemmings in full daylight, so she declared that they must go immediately.

Ofred cringed and gave a little whine as he dropped to the ground in the midst of the lemmings. His red eyes shone with madness, and Little Fur's heart sank. Yet there was nothing for it but to begin the journey.

They moved more swiftly than Little Fur had hoped. The lemmings swarmed, which meant they could draw upon the power of the horde to strengthen them. And for all his oddness, Ofred had a rapid gait. Even Little Fur moved faster than usual, for there  was no need to make sure she set her feet down on grass or earth. Knowing this, Crow led them in a very direct route toward the river. All of them were alert for greeps and humans.

They passed into the part of the city where the high houses clustered thickly, a few pale stars reflected in their shining surfaces. Little Fur had never been here before, because there were so few trees and plants. She gazed up at the forest of darkly gleaming high houses and saw a chilly beauty in them, for all their deadness. She shuddered, wondering if this was a sign that her troll blood was growing stronger.

Crow led them across a wide square made of shining blocks of polished stone. Not a single blade of grass grew between the blocks. At the center of the square was a great stone bowl from which sprang the likenesses of four enormous rearing white horses, their faces frozen in straining desperation. Little Fur did not know why humans would shape stones in such ways, but they must possess a kind of magic to capture such urgency in stone. Water flowed from under the horses as if they were leaping up out of it, but it smelled of human poisons, so none of them drank from it, though they were thirsty.

The sky grew lighter, and soon only one bright star remained. Little Fur's legs were weary, for she was not used to walking so fast. She wanted to ask Crow how much farther the river was, but summoning him would waste time. It was strange to think that this was how humans went through their cities, striding about without fear.

She had once asked Crow how he knew where she could walk safely when he was flying above the city. He had said that birds saw the earth magic as a shimmer of green, flowing like a stream and pooling around trees and gardens and patches of grass. Crow had also told her that birds saw the air currents as shimmering golden paths, and that those birds who flew away for the winter used them to find their way home in spring.

I ought to feel free, Little Fur thought, but when she passed a stunted tree and couldn't reach down through its roots to commune with the seven ancient sentinels in her beloved wilderness, she felt alone.

The last star winked out as they passed from the high houses to the outer limits of the city. There the empty dwellings were smaller, with patches of grass and more trees. Crow flew lower now and circled often, for he knew, as all of them did, that this area was where greeps were more likely to hide. Crow led them to a narrow, shadowy lane, and the lemmings funneled into it after Little Fur and Ofred.

Little Fur had not gone far along it when one of the shadows rose and took a solid shape. Little Fur reeled back with a cry of fright as an enormous black cat emerged from the gloom.

"Danger," she whispered.

It was the panther that Sly had vowed to free from the zoo: Danger, who had sworn his own oath to kill and kill if he was freed. Crow plummeted out of the night sky, silent as a stone, claws outstretched. But he was not an owl with silent wings, and the rush of air warned the great cat. He leaped sideways and pounced on the black bird, pinning him under one powerful dark paw.

"No!" said Ofred.

Little Fur gaped as the lemur laid his small paw on the panther's large one and said softly, "I did not dream of you killing."

Danger held the lemur's gaze, then sheathed his claws and lifted his paw. Freed, Crow fluttered upright and flew up to the top of a pole topped with a ball of false light, where he began a scolding tirade.

Little Fur ignored him, asking the lemur, "What happened at the zoo?"

It was Danger who answered. "The cat Sly stole the key and then freed the lemur from his enclosure so that he could open my cage." He turned back to Ofred. "Did you speak the truth, dreamer?" he demanded.

"I told you my dream. You will not be free unless you travel with me," sang Ofred, the fire fading in his eyes.

Danger turned to Little Fur, then looked over at the lemmings. They all watched him with grave, respectful eyes. "These are also following you?" Danger asked Ofred at last, disdainfully.

"They have chosen to follow my dreams, as you may do," answered the lemming. "I alone cannot choose."

"I—I don't understand," Little Fur stammered at Danger. "You are free."

The panther looked at her for a long moment before deigning to answer. "I was trapped in this shape when humans captured and caged me. I wore it so long that I had forgotten myself. The moment I was outside my cage, I remembered myself. But my flesh has forgotten how to shift."

"You are a shapeshifter?" Little Fur murmured, for she could smell nothing of the last age in the great dark beast.

"I was. Perhaps I will be again. But this shape goes deep." There was a rumble in the panther's throat, and he regarded Ofred suspiciously.

The lemur was humming a tuneless little song and preening the bedraggled tip of his tail.

Little Fur looked up at the lightening sky. "Listen, Ofred has dreamed of the great sea, and that is where we are going. We will follow the river to

94

it, but we must get outside the city before the sun opens its eye. If you would come with us, then come, else the humans will see us."

"I will not be caged again," Danger said. "Let us go."

Little Fur looked up and nodded to Crow, who flew on just above the lane. Danger leaped after him and the lemmings swarmed in Danger's wake, leaving Little Fur and Ofred to bring up the rear. It seemed to her that the lemur was moving more slowly. No doubt he was weary, too. As soon as they reached the river and got out of the city, they would rest and forage for some food.

Little Fur was about to ask Danger what had happened to Sly when Crow screamed a warning: "Humans coming!"

CHAPTER 7
The Wander

Little Fur looked around in dismay. The lane was narrow and there was nowhere to hide, except for an enormous metal bin set in a niche in a wall ahead. "We must hide behind that," she cried, but already Danger was weaving cat shadow about himself.

Little Fur turned and ran toward the metal box, gagging at the awful smell rising from it. The lemmings flowed in a soft tide under and behind it. Just as Little Fur was about to press herself in beside them, she realized that the lemur was sitting on his haunches in the middle of the lane, gazing vacantly into the false light.

And now Little Fur could *hear* the humans!

She ran back, grabbed Ofred's paw, and dragged him into the malodorous space behind the metal box. Sinking into a crouch, she put her arms about him and whispered that he must be quiet. He trembled, but made no sound.

Little Fur could see the hulking shapes of the humans coming along the lane. There were three of them, and they were reeling as they walked. Little Fur could smell the sickly sweet smell of fermented fruit coming from them, and realized that one of them was almost a greep.

To Little Fur's horror, one of the

humans stopped alongside the metal box and heaved it open with a screeching creak. There was a shout from one of the other humans, and the rummaging one dropped the lid with a clang and stumped angrily to where they were doing something to the wall. There were long hissing sounds and a terrible smell—but at last the humans staggered on, leaving strange glistening runes on the wall.

Little Fur breathed a shuddering sigh of relief as Crow glided down to land on the metal box. "Run! To escape from Danger will be easy now!" he cawed urgently.

Before Little Fur could speak, something black landed beside him. Crow screamed in fright and took to the air, but Little Fur saw at once that it was only Sly. "I am so glad to see you!" she said.

The one-eyed cat gave her a green and glowing look, then leaped to the ground, where Danger was emerging from the cat shadow he had woven. "I followed your scent," she told Danger. "You will go with the lemur?"

"He said that things were not as they seemed, and that was true," Danger told her.

"He smells of madness," Sly said disdainfully.

"Yes," Danger replied. "It is that which made me change my mind. For madness does not come from lies. It comes from too much truth."

"You could remain in this shape. It is strong and powerful," Sly said lightly, as if it did not matter to her at all what he chose to do.

"This shape is beautiful, but it is another cage. I must be free. You made me know that, Emerald Eye."

Sly said nothing, and Danger bent down to touch noses with her. They exchanged a long look; then, suddenly, Danger stiffened. Both cats turned their bright gazes back to the lane.

"Must going!" cawed Crow, circling overhead. "Sun will soon opening its eye!"

Sly stretched and yawned before bidding them all farewell and leaping up over the wall.

"Go!" Little Fur commanded the lemmings, and they swarmed along the lane. She looked at

Ofred, who sat where she had left him, sucking his fingers. She sighed and took his wet paw, but before they could go more than two steps, Danger blocked their way.

Little Fur thought that the panther meant to attack, but he merely said, in his low, smoky voice, "I will carry him."

Little Fur nodded and pushed the lemur up onto the huge cat's back. Ofred hardly seemed aware of what was happening to him, though she heard him mutter, "Who will ride upon the back of Danger must beware its teeth and claws. . . ."

They set off again. The lane spilled into a wider cobbled street with a gutter cut down the center. Even as Danger loped after Crow, the sun began to open its eye. They had a little time, for the sun had to reach over the roofs before they would be completely exposed. Now Little Fur could smell a large body of water ahead. A moment later, she heard the cry of birds and saw a flock of them wheeling around Crow in a pattern that told her they were exchanging news.

As she waited below, Little Fur found herself fingering the green stone hanging from her neck. She lifted the stone and examined it closely, searching for a tiny fissure or crack where something might be hidden. She wondered what it

was that trolls did not like about the feel of earth magic and shivered at the thought that a day might come when she was not just numb to the earth spirit, but repelled by it. It struck her that right now she was not like a troll or an elf; she was most like a human, because she could walk anywhere and feel nothing.

Crow dropped away from the flock and swooped low, cawing, "River being right ahead!"

They had not gone far before a high metal web that stretched out of sight in both directions blocked the way. Little Fur wrestled with a surge of anger at the thought that, once again, humans had spoiled things.

Crow cawed that he would fly along the fence to seek a place where they could get through it or under it, and then he was gone.

"I can jump it," Danger said. "I will carry the lemur over, and you and the lemmings can climb it."

"That would not be wise," said a gruff, shaggy sort of voice.

Little Fur turned to see a very hairy creature coming toward them. It looked like a big dog but smelled strongly of the age of high magic. Ofred seemed not to notice the creature, but the lemmings sniffed and stared at it with interest.

"Do not try to stop us!" Danger snarled, baring his teeth.

"I would not dream of it," the creature said with a chuckle. "I am only warning you that the fence will give you a powerful shock if you touch it, because it is full of sky-fire."

"We must get to the river," said Little Fur, knowing they could not tamper with sky-fire. "How far does the fence go?"

"You'd have to walk a long, weary way before you could get around it to the riverbank," answered the creature.

"What is caged by this web?" Danger asked.

"Only the humans know that," said the creature. Little Fur smelled that whatever else he was, he was male. "Do you mind which bank of the river?"

"What do you mean?" asked Little Fur.

"Well, there is a bridge that goes from this side of the fence right over the web and across to the other bank. And there is no fence on that side. I can show it to you if you like."

"That would be wonderful," Little Fur said. Crow could easily follow, she told herself, and there was no time to spare.

They had not walked far before Little Fur saw the bridge. It was slender, far too narrow and light for road beasts.

"What are you, and what is your name?" Little Fur asked the doglike creature as they neared the bridge.

"I am Wander," her guide said, giving her a look that glimmered with amusement. "That is what I am and who I am, and also what I do."

Little Fur had never heard of a wander before, but there were many creatures from the last age she did not know about. She introduced Danger and Ofred and the lemming horde. The lemmings bowed gravely, and the wander inclined his own head with the same gravity, though there was a twinkle of amusement in his eye.

"How do you know the web is so long?" the panther asked, his fur still prickling suspiciously.

"I went both ways to see how long it was," explained the wander.

"You did all that walking out of curiosity?" Little Fur asked.

"That is what I do," said the creature. "I wander when I wonder."

"It must take you a long time to get anywhere," Little Fur said.

"There is no hurry to get where I am going, since it is the same place we are all going in the end," answered Wander. "On the other hand, there is a great herd of things to wonder about on my way to join the world's dream, and when a question starts niggling at me, I go wandering until I find the answer and stop wondering. Or until some other question starts nagging at me more."

Little Fur imagined questions coming to Wander like small creatures came to her. "I suppose you brought us to the bridge because you were wondering about us," she said.

The wander chuckled. "I thought you smelled clever. I *am* curious about why three such different kinds of creature travel together with a horde of lemmings. I can't think of any question that you might share."

"Are you asking me what we are doing?" Little Fur asked.

Wander gave her a long look out of eyes that were the exact shade of honeycomb. "A wondering that is answered by someone else is like a nut that is eaten by someone else; all you have is an empty shell. Besides, hardly anyone knows the true reason for doing a thing."

Little Fur was about to say crossly that she knew very well what she was doing, until it struck her that she knew only that they were to go to the great sea.

Crow landed and began scolding Little Fur:

"What you are thinking, going over bridgeness without Crow to flying ahead?"

Little Fur let him splutter into silence, then told him the new plan and introduced him to Wander. Slightly mollified, Crow flew off, insisting that he must make sure no humans lurked at the other end of the bridge.

"The bird is bound to you," observed Wander.

"We are bound to one another," Little Fur told him, surprised that he had been able to smell the link between them.

By the time they reached the other end of the bridge, the sun was shining on them. Little Fur could see through the veils of morning mist that the river's course was far from straight. "How far must we walk along the bank before the river leaves the city?" she asked Wander.

"Will you go downstream or upstream?"

"Downstream," Little Fur said. "We are going to follow the river to the great sea."

"A full day of walking will see you clear of the city, and two days more will get you beyond human farms that surround the city where the river flows," answered Wander promptly. Then he glanced at the lemmings flowing about the feet of the lemur. "But it is a long, wearisome walk from there to the great sea."

Little Fur's heart sank. "We will have to find somewhere to hide until it is dark again."

"If you are in a hurry to get out of the city, you

might travel in a road serpent," suggested Wander. "There is a feeding station not far from here. You could even ride in one all the way to the great sea."

"A road serpent!" Little Fur said in astonishment. "But humans ride inside their bellies."

"They do, but there are always empty places. I ought to know, for I have traveled in them more than once, sometimes with a human and sometimes alone."

"You traveled with humans?" Little Fur said, shocked. Danger, walking on the elf troll's other side, gave the wander a glare of mistrust.

"Only with humans who can feel the earth spirit," he said.

Little Fur stared at him in disbelief. "I have never heard of a human that could feel the flow of earth magic," she finally managed to say.

"Humans do not feel it," snarled Danger. "How could they?"

"Well, they don't feel it all the time, and those that do are always very old or very young," conceded the wander, but absentmindedly, as if some new question were tugging at him. Then he said, "The road-serpent feeding station is down-river, so you won't need to make up your mind until you get there. And if you don't want to go in a road serpent after all, the feeding station will be a good place to hide for the day."

As they hurried along the river, keeping to the shadows as much as they could, Danger asked Wander how they could be sure the road serpent they rode in would take them to the great sea.

"I know from experience which road serpent will go near to the seacoast and slow down enough so you can jump right off," the wander replied.

This sounded terribly dangerous, but the wander insisted he had done it before. "You just need to jump when I tell you."

Little Fur stared at him in surprise. "You will come with us?"

"I have no choice, because meeting you and your friends has made me immensely curious," he said comfortably.

The sun was high by the time they reached the road-serpent feeding station. Fortunately, the metal web that surrounded it contained no sky-fire, and it was so old and buckled that all of them except Danger could easily creep under it. He simply leaped over it, with Ofred clinging to his back.

Once they had got past the web and the lines of sheds, they all stopped in awe of the many sleek metal serpents that stood side by side on their rails. Even Ofred seemed to come out of his daze as Little Fur helped him down from Danger's back, and he gave a soft whimper of fear. Immediately the nearest lemmings responded by moving closer and pressing themselves around him. As ever, he seemed unaware of their attention, though he did sit back on his haunches and begin to chew his paws.

"The road serpents sleep," Danger said, but there was a growl in his voice and his fur pricked and gave off sparks.

"They do not truly sleep or live," the wander

told him. "They are machines made by humans. There are devices in them that force them to go or stop, which humans operate."

Crow flapped down to land at the top of a pole and asked crossly, "Why we are coming to this place?"

Little Fur told him the wander's suggestion, still trying to take in what the wander had said about the road serpents.

Crow screeched and ranted until Danger snarled, "I will eat you if you do not be silent!"

Crow gave him an affronted look and flew off in a huff, muttering that someone had to keep watch for humans, since everyone else was clearly mad or stupid. Little Fur sighed, knowing that he was being difficult partly because his role had been usurped by the wander, and partly because he knew he would not be able to fly fast enough to keep up with a road serpent.

"I will show you the road serpent that goes toward the great sea," said the wander. He led Little Fur, Danger, Ofred and the lemmings over

113

several sets of silver rails laid on crushed stone, and around patches where no grass grew. The lemmings gave a wide berth to the rails, and Little Fur knew they could smell the poisons humans used to prevent plants from growing there. She stepped very carefully, having been stung by the poisons before.

"This is the one we must take," said Wander as they reached a massive yellow road serpent sleeping upon its rails. He continued along the length of the monster, adding, "This is not a road serpent for carrying humans. Only a few of them go in the very front. The rest of the serpent is filled with boxes and barrels. We have only to find a place that is not full."

There were great doors in the side of each section of the road serpent, which made the sections seem less like live beasts and more like human dwellings on wheels. Little Fur and Wander moved along the side of the road serpent, peering into the open doors, but the lemmings, too small to see in, remained clustered about Ofred. Danger drifted in the other direction along the same side of the road serpent, his tail snaking and coiling. It did not take long for the wander to find a section that was more than half empty with its ramp down.

"We can ride right in here, comfy as fleas on a dog," Wander said.

Suddenly they heard a loud yowl and a guttural shriek coming from behind them. Little Fur and the wander hastened back along the side of the train to where the lemmings and Ofred were waiting, all of them gazing in the other direction.

"Where is Danger?" Little Fur whispered.

"He went into the shadows there," said one of the lemmings, pointing at a pool of shadow between two shacks built between the rails.

Then they heard a shriek of terror, which was abruptly cut off.

"Troll," said the wander thoughtfully. "I smell troll."

CHAPTER 8
The Road Serpent

Danger padded out of the shadows. To Little Fur's surprise, Sly was with him! Then she saw that they carried a lumpy, unconscious body of a small troll between them.

"It was following you," Sly told Little Fur. "I had to hunt slowly, else it would have slipped down a cranny and away."

Little Fur looked into the twisted face of the troll, realizing that *this* was the reason for the purposeful look the two cats had exchanged earlier.

"You hunted well, Emerald Eye," said Danger approvingly.

"We brought it so that you could see it," Sly told Little Fur. "Now we will kill it."

"No!" said Little Fur. One part of her felt so angry at being followed that she wanted to strike out at the troll, but still, she had never hit anything in her life, much less caused death.

The wander gave a polite sort of cough and said, "No goodly thing ever came of killing unless it protected kin or staved off starvation."

"I do not think the troll meant to hurt me," Little Fur said, touching the green stone hanging from her neck. "It was trying to steal this for the Troll King, though I do not know why he would want it so badly."

"The troll was ssspying," Sly hissed angrily. "It heard everything. If you let it live, it will return to the Troll King and tell all!"

"Tie up troll and leaving it for humans to finding," Crow advised.

Little Fur shook her head. "That would be the same as killing it. But it must be held captive until I return from this quest." She thought for a time. "I have some seeds in my cloak that will make the troll sleep for a day," she said. "We can carry it into one of these huts, where the smell of human is old. Then Crow must fly back to Tillet and ask her to organize some creatures to fetch the troll back to the wilderness before it wakes up." Little Fur looked at Crow. "Tell her the troll must not be harmed, but neither must it be allowed to escape. We will let it go after I return."

"Crow will not leaving Little Fur," Crow said stubbornly.

"Crow, I need you to let Tillet know about the troll. And Sorrow might need your help in finding Nobody," Little Fur said firmly. "Besides, you must find Ginger and tell him that I have gone away in a road serpent."

"Why cannot *Sly* doing these tellings?" Crow cawed. Little Fur saw the alarm behind his sullenness.

"I am a hunter, and I do not deliver messages," Sly said haughtily. "Besides, I have some spying of my own to do. I will go to Underth and find out why the Troll King wants Little Fur's own special stone." There was a gleam of wicked daring in her green eye.

Crow glared. "That being stupidest idea!" he said coldly. He clacked his beak and puffed up his chest as he always did when he was composing a very important message. "Crow will telling all things and doing what is needing to do. But when telling and doing are done, Crow will flying after yellow road serpent." He gave Wander and Danger each a hard look, as if to make sure they understood that he did not trust them.

Little Fur gathered Crow into her arms, even though she knew it would upset his dignity, and pressed her face to his sleek blue-black head. She sniffed up the feathery black smell of him before releasing him. He cried, "Nevermore!" and flew up into the sky.

Little Fur watched until he was gone from

sight. Then she turned to Sly. "You must not go to Underth. You told me yourself that the Troll King suspects traitors ever since we escaped from his dungeons."

"I am not afraid of the Troll King," Sly said, her long tail lashing back and forth. There was no use arguing. The black cat stretched languidly, cast one burning look at Danger, and bounded out of sight.

Sighing, Little Fur dug some seeds from a pocket in her cloak. Both Wander and Danger watched with interest while she ground them between two stones. The lemmings were grazing on weeds and grasses, while Ofred continued to sit, half dozing and muttering to himself, arms outstretched as if to embrace the sunlight.

Little Fur looked down into the small troll's face. Then she knelt and began to feed the powder into his wide mouth, rubbing his throat to make him swallow. While touching him, she realized, as she had the one time she had touched a human, that one sleeping creature was much the same as another. If she closed her eyes, she might have been touching a rough place on her own skin, or any animal.

Little Fur coaxed the powder into the sleeping troll. Then she, Danger and Wander dragged it into a shed that was gray with age and festooned with spiderwebs. Ofred skittered after them to watch. Little Fur was just tucking a handful of valuable web into her cloak when another dreadful shrill scream filled the air.

Danger and the lemur threw themselves to the ground. Little Fur cringed and clapped her hands over her ears. The wander did not react at all, save to start slightly. There was yet another dreadful scream; then the yellow metal road serpent began to groan and shudder.

"The road serpent will go soon," Wander announced cheerfully. "We had better get into it now."

"You can swarm up the planks," Little Fur told the lemmings, but none of them moved. One of the lemmings stepped forward. She wasn't a teta, for she was too young, but there was an air of certainty about her that belied her small, sleek dark form.

"Healer, my name is Silk. I must tell you that some of the lemmings will come with you, but many will remain, for the territory of the old clan ended on the other side of the river. Some wish to start a new clan here."

"But there are humans here," Little Fur said.

"There are humans almost everywhere," Silk said solemnly. "And where they are not, they will someday go."

"The Sett Owl said you ought to follow Ofred to your territory," Little Fur said, worried for the small creatures, for surely a yard where road serpents slept was not a safe place for a territory.

"Healer, the Sett Owl said that those who follow the lemur to the end will find a wondrous territory, but not all lemmings desire wondrousness," Silk said.

"Will you come?" asked Little Fur curiously.

"I will follow the lemur to the end," said Silk;

then she bowed and went and tugged at Ofred's paw, leading him to the place where lemmings were still swarming aboard. Those lemmings staying bowed low to Little Fur and to Ofred, and melted away. Little Fur sighed and went with Wander and Danger to board as well.

Inside the section, a pile of barrels and boxes was lashed down, with quite a lot of space behind and beside them. Many of the lemmings found nooks and crannies to hide in. The rest, including Silk, made way for the lemur, who curled up to sleep, and then they settled closely around him.

Little Fur went back to the opening, where Danger and Wander sat, gazing out. The road serpent's groans and wheezes increased. All at once, Little Fur heard a human voice! Little Fur, Danger, Sly and the unhidden lemmings hastened into the shadows as the voice came closer.

There was a long rasping sound, followed by a great bang. This sound repeated, and Little Fur realized that the humans were shutting doors in the side of the road serpent. She trembled with indecision, knowing that if they were locked in, they would not be able to jump out when the road serpent reached the great sea.

Then a human appeared at the opening, lifted the ramp, and slid it into the floor with a bang. At that very moment, the lemur gave a loud moan.

There was a listening silence and the human clambered inside, giving off a smell of suspicion and aggression as it moved toward them. Danger gave a low, savage growl. The human froze and began to impart the sharp stink of fear. But before it or Danger could do anything, Wander got to his feet and trotted out from behind the pile of boxes toward the human, wagging his tail.

The human stared at the wander. Little Fur held her breath. All at once the human's scent changed to surprise and relief, and it bent down and held out its hand. Little Fur watched in amazement as the wander sniffed the human's hand and then licked it! The human gave a shout of pleased laughter and called out to another human. The new one put its head in the opening.

When it saw Wander, it, too, held out its hand for Wander to smell and lick.

The two humans began to talk earnestly. Little Fur could sense that they were trying to make up their minds what to do about the wander. Their words smelled of kindness and also impatience; then, slowly, came another scent. It was an aroma of calmness, mingled with something like the sweet scent given off by any animal mothering its young. It was coming from the wander. The talk of the humans slowed, then faltered, and then they simply left off stroking him and went on their way, leaving the door open.

"What did you do to them?" Little Fur asked Wander.

"I soothed them," he answered, as if it had been nothing at all.

The road serpent gave another long, tortured scream. It shuddered and began to move along its rails with a slow clackety-clack. The serpent gathered speed, and the sound went faster, too. The wind blustered through the opening, tangling

Little Fur's hair and making her cloak flutter wildly. Rather than taking shelter, she wrapped her cloak tightly about her and went to sit closer to the opening, staring out at the strange sight of human houses and roads, and at clumps of trees flashing by.

Soon the road serpent was racing through open country. Little Fur saw human farms surrounded by the maze of fences humans used to mark their territory. Then there were fewer and fewer of these until there was only a vast plain covered in tall grasses that bowed down at their passing. Above this marvelous flat green, the sky arched like an immense blue gourd.

In the afternoon, the road serpent plunged into a valley where a dark forest grew. Little Fur sniffed with delight at the scents of so many trees, wishing she might commune with them. She felt a movement and turned to see Ofred beside her. She was fearful that he might speak of some dream that had come to him, but he only gazed out, as she was doing.

After a time, the wander came to sit with Little Fur and Ofred. "The lemmings have told me that you are seeking the earth spirit," he said.

"Yes, I have been cut off from the flow of earth magic," said Little Fur. "The Sett Owl told me that if I would rejoin the flow, I must follow Ofred's dreams and they would lead me to the source."

"The Sett Owl," murmured Wander slowly, as if he were tasting the flavor of the name. "Do you know, it was the Sett Owl who set me to traveling in the first place. There was a great restlessness of questions in me, and when I heard talk of a seer living in a beaked house, I went and made my offering. The Sett Owl said there was no cure for such curiosity. Indeed, she seemed to think it a gift rather than a burden. She said that I ought to try wandering while I wondered, because at least that would use up the restlessness. I have been wandering and wondering ever since." He was silent for a while; then he glanced at Ofred, who had fallen into a doze again.

"The lemmings said *he* was their guide," the wander murmured.

"The Sett Owl told them that if they followed Ofred, they would find the new territory they need, and that those who followed him to the end would find a strange and wondrous home. But I think lemmings are not much interested in strangeness." Little Fur looked at Ofred. "It is hard to believe that the dreams of one small lemur can lead the lemmings to a new territory, as well as remind Danger how to shapeshift *and* bring me to the earth spirit."

"That explains why he smells of madness," said Wander. "It is a hard thing to live a life led by dreams."

The shadows were long when the road serpent slowed down and began to struggle up a steep incline that brought them out of the valley and back onto the grassy plain. The rails curved inland slightly for a time, and Little Fur caught a glimpse of the cloudlike ice mountains far away on the horizon. They made her think of Nobody and wonder what was happening to her. Little Fur could not imagine Sorrow failing to rescue her.

"Do you remember anything of your past?" Wander asked Danger as they all sat together in the thin sunlight that shone through the ragged clouds fleeting across the sky. The day was coming to a close, and the road serpent was now traveling over stony broken flatlands. The wind was strong, and damp with the promise of rain.

"I remember a hot, wet land," said Danger. He was stretched out full-length, his black chin resting on his crossed paws. "I saw a black shape full of deadliness that was as graceful as flowing water. I wanted to know how it would feel to be so soft and yet so deadly, so I took its shape. That is when the humans caught me in their nets. They caged me, and I forgot the truth of myself. I knew only a savage boredom that made me want to kill. I did not remember what I was until Sly freed me."

"Why did she free you?" wondered Wander.

"I do not know," Danger said. "I meant to kill her, for she taunted me and called me a fool and a coward when I would not help her to free me. She clawed at me with her words until I told her all I knew about the she-human who had the key to my cage. Once Sly had stolen the key, neither of us could use it. So Sly went to get a monkey, but when she came back, the lemur was with her. I would like to know why she freed me. When I return, I will ask her."

The pace of the road serpent changed, and the swift clackety-clack became a slower click-click-clack, click-click-clack. The wander rose. "We must ready ourselves for the leap from the road serpent's belly," he announced.

Heart hammering, Little Fur shook the lemur awake. He flinched from her hands, his red eyes shining with madness and confusion. Then Little Fur began to rouse the lemmings, urging them to waken others. At last they were all gathered by the opening.

As the train continued to slow, Wander said Danger must go first with Ofred on his back; then the lemmings should go in waves. Last of all, he and Little Fur would jump together. "When I say 'go,' there must be no hesitation," he warned. "Anyone jumping too late will be killed, for the train speeds up again."

Little Fur was growing more and more nervous, but she was puzzled, too, because there was no sign of the great sea. Smelling her question, the wander said, "After the stone hills come the sand dunes, and then there is the sea. The rails do not go into the dunes, so we must jump onto the sand and walk the rest of the way."

As the train slowed almost to a stop at a sharp bend, Wander barked, "Go!" Danger leaped. Then the lemmings leaped, in wave after wave. Finally, only Wander and Little Fur were left.

"Quick!" Wander said, and he jumped.

Little Fur swallowed a great choking lump of terror, thought of Sorrow, and jumped after him. There was an endless moment in which she flew — or fell — through nothing. Then her head hit something hard and the world went dark.

CHAPTER 9
The Salten Sea

Little Fur awoke to the sound of a great muffled roaring. The light in the clouds above was that of the end of the day. The wander was sitting beside her, but there was no sign of Ofred or Danger or the lemmings.

"Where are the others?" she asked, struggling to sit up.

"You knocked your head on a stone when you landed," Wander said. "Danger and the lemmings have gone to the shore of the sea. Do you want to go down to them?"

"What is that noise?" asked Little Fur, standing up.

"It is the great sea," Wander said.

"The *sea*?" Little Fur cried in astonishment.

Instead of speaking, the wander began to make his way up the white dunes, avoiding the long whipping strands of sea grass. Little Fur got to her feet and followed him. The sand was far softer than the little patches of coarse sand in the wilderness, and it squeaked under her feet. But then she reached the top of a rise and the sight of the great sea drove all else from her mind. Water ran from the land to the horizon before her, and the immensity of it seemed to speak some truth too huge for any single creature to understand.

Brownie had spoken of waves, but none of his stories had prepared her for their huge, murmurous thunder or their compelling rhythm. In the fading light, Little Fur watched as the edge of the sea heaved up into a wave that toppled forward, curling with white foam as it crashed down upon

134

the sand. Then it dragged itself massively back, drawing sand and weed and pebbles with it, leaving a spittle of foam hissing in its wake, only to thump down again. The movement was so enormous that Little Fur felt herself  swaying, first toward the retreating sea, and then away as it roared back to her.

Little Fur stood staring at the sea for a long time, the sticky dampness of the night air settling on her skin like wet spiderweb. At last she roused herself and looked along the shore, seeking the others. In one direction, the edge of the land stretched away to vanishing in a pale curve. In the other direction, there was an outcrop of black rocks, rising up against the velvet dimness of the clouded evening.

It was several moments before Little Fur saw that Danger and Ofred were sitting on top of the rocks. Little Fur called out to them, and Danger leaped onto the sand and padded over to her. Ofred remained where he was, peering out at the horizon. A few of the lemmings were perched on the rocks around the lemur, watching him.

"What is happening?" she shouted over the noise.

"Ofred dreamed of waiting on the rocks," Danger said.

Little Fur felt a flicker of anger, but she was too weary to fight. "I don't suppose he dreamed what we are waiting for?" she asked.

"A gift," Danger said. "A gift and a way."

As night settled in, most of the older lemmings went off to explore the mild land leading up to the seashore. It was green and inviting, and it seemed not to be the territory of any other animal for whom the lemmings might be prey. Wander went with them, saying that he would forage for food and find a source of water.

Danger had told Little Fur that Ofred's dream had included both himself and Little Fur, so Little Fur had spread out her father's cloak on the dry sand farther up the beach and sat down to wait. Danger lay down beside her and fell asleep. Watching how the sea heaved and boiled in a ceaseless echo of the roiling clouds overhead, Little Fur felt dizzy and half hypnotized. She lay back on the cool sand beside Danger.

Her thoughts drifted to Ginger and Crow, whose absence tugged at the link between them. She thought of Nobody in a cage somewhere; of Sly slinking down to spy on the Troll King; of the poor harling trapped under the round house; of Gem, who had taken on the terrible responsibility of becoming the Sett Owl; of Tillet the hare, guarding the small troll held captive in the wilderness, and of the seven ancient trees that kept the wilderness safe. She wondered yet again what the Troll King wanted with her green stone and if there was truly any real hope of finding the earth spirit.

Without warning, Danger leaped into the air with a yowl.

Little Fur sat up and found that the sea had crept darkly up the sand, almost to her toes. The panther stood just above the waterline, shaking his wet paws in disgust. As Little Fur got to her feet, the clouds parted to reveal the arching vault of the night sky and its swirling glitter of stars just as the moon was rising. Little Fur caught her breath, for the moon was the same mad red as the lemur's dreaming eyes. Then she saw that the rising moon had burnished a red-gold path on the heaving darkness of the sea, a path that ran all the way from the distant horizon to her own feet.

"What is *that*?" the panther murmured, curiosity in his smoky voice. He had come to stand beside Little Fur.

Little Fur looked at him, puzzled, but then she saw that he was not looking up at the moon. She followed the direction of his gaze and saw what had caught his attention: something dark and large and strangely shaped was moving along the shining moon path in the great sea.

Little Fur tried to make out what sort of creature it was as it slowly came nearer. It seemed to her that it was not so much swimming as floating. It bobbed and drifted closer, vanishing occasionally behind a wave. All at once, Little Fur understood that it was not a creature she was seeing, but a tree—uprooted and floating in the water, its branches rising up at one end and its root net at the other. There was something caught in the branches, and the closer the dead tree floated, the more it looked to Little Fur as if a large white sheet of ice was wedged there.

Surely ice would melt? she thought. *I must be mistaken.*

A movement caught her eye, and she saw that Ofred had risen up onto his hind legs, with his arms outstretched. He had either not noticed or did not care that the water was still rising! Little Fur ran toward the half-submerged isthmus of rocks, which was all that now connected his rocky island to the sandy shore.

"Ofred!" Little Fur shouted.

Instead of answering her, Ofred lowered his arms, stepped forward, and vanished!

Little Fur gasped and clambered over the slippery black rocks until she reached the place where the lemur had been sitting. It overlooked a wedge-shaped inlet, which was not visible except from directly above it. Several lemmings were making their way down to where the lemur was perched on a narrow ledge jutting out from the side of the inlet.

As Little Fur climbed very carefully after them, she glanced out to sea. The moon path had shifted and led directly into the inlet. And the floating tree had turned and was coming toward the inlet, roots first, as if it meant to plant itself sideways into the land.

"The gift must be taken before it is withdrawn," Ofred chanted feverishly, stretching out his black paws.

Little Fur noticed in alarm that the tree had begun to drift to one side, and would miss the inlet gap. Without thinking, she plunged into the water. It was far deeper than she was tall, and she went under into the gritty churn of the tide. To her amazement, she discovered that although earth magic did not flow through the great sea, *some other potent force did!*

Little Fur was astounded at the sheer strength of the power raging about her. She thought again of Ofred's words: The gift must be taken before it is withdrawn. Ignoring the salt water trying to force its way down her throat, she threw out her hands again and again, her feet naturally treading water and holding her up. She moved forward until she caught two solid fistfuls of stiff tree roots.

Little Fur could feel the power in the water tugging at the tree, which was now loosely wedged at the mouth of the inlet. Her trollish stubbornness gave her the courage to find a foothold against the stone and hold the tree in its position so that it could not be sucked out and away. Then a wave washed in and pushed the tree straight into the inlet, wedging it firmly in place. Gasping, Little Fur paddled back to the stone ledge, where several of the younger lemmings waited.

Little Fur dragged herself up onto the ledge and saw that Ofred had leaped onto the tree. He ran along its gnarled and pitted trunk to its branches, where the white thing that Little Fur had thought was ice was jammed. The notice was some sort of flat, smooth, human-made stuff. It was lodged in the branches along with tufts of grass and other human debris.

"What is it?" Danger demanded, looking down from the rocks.

"It is flotsam," said Silk, who was among the lemmings who had remained with Ofred.

"It is the way," sang the lemur. He looked miserable.

"You dreamed of the tree?" Little Fur asked Ofred.

"I dreamed of riding upon it."

"Upon?" Little Fur echoed. "You dreamed of yourself riding on the tree?"

"I saw us. We three," Ofred said, and his eyes went from Little Fur up to Danger. "And the small ones." He looked down at Silk and the other lemmings. Then he turned to the sea. "Out there," he added, almost absently.

CHAPTER 10
Flotsam

"The tree can be a raft!" said Wander enthusiastically. He had returned from his foraging with several of the lemmings.

The lemmings had come to bid Little Fur and Ofred farewell on behalf of the rest. Most of them had decided to remain and make the safe, sandy shore their new territory.

"What is a raft?" Little Fur asked, the tips of her ears tingling at the peculiar perilous odor of the word. She was afraid that she already knew the answer.

"A raft is something that can be ridden over water. I knew a human youngling who made one from a small piece of this white stuff caught in the branches, and set it forth on the great sea. Perhaps it floats still. You will need a sail to catch the wind, so that it will move," he added thoughtfully. "Your cloak will serve, Little Fur. It can be tied among the branches to catch the wind." He looked at her and smiled. "Humans are always traveling over the great sea on road beasts that float."

Little Fur looked at Ofred, who had returned to sit on the ledge. He was rocking back and forth, occasionally swatting at the air as if fending off an invisible flying creature. Whenever his gaze fell on the sea, he shivered and chewed at his tail. Silk and the other lemmings who would follow him until the end remained faithfully by his side, grooming him.

As for Danger, the shapeshifter was regarding the tufted tree and its slab of white stuff with loathing, black ears flat to his skull. Even his long, elegant tail was fluffed.

Never were three less likely creatures supposed to journey, Little Fur thought with despair, turning to Ofred again. "You truly dreamed this? That we must ride on this out on the sea, and that it will bring us to the earth spirit?"

The lemur looked into her eyes. "I dreamed that we will give ourselves to the sea."

Little Fur, not liking the sound of that at all, licked her lips, which tasted of tears. "Did you see where the sea will bring us? Do we come safe to land?"

"We will come safe to ground, but beyond that land is the most dangerous place of all, for it is the maw of the great sea." He shivered, closed his eyes, and began rocking back and forth again, singing softly to himself.

Despite her frustration, Little Fur felt a surge of pity for the small tormented beast. He had spoken the truth when he said that they could choose whether or not to follow his dreams, but he had no choice about dreaming. The anger she had felt cooled, for what choice, truly, did she have either?

Danger hissed and leaped down the rocks to the sandy shore. Little Fur followed to where he waited on the sand, his eyes two blazing yellow slits. He bared his teeth at her; they were white and sharp and long.

"I cannot do this," he snarled.

"A cat could not," she told him, "but you are not truly a cat."

The panther reared up. "What use will it be to find I can shift shapes if I am only to choose the shape in which to die?" he demanded fiercely.

"Ofred did not dream that we would die," Little Fur said. "He dreamed that if we three went, we would come safe to land."

"He said that beyond the land, which is not safe, is the most dangerous place of all," said Danger. "He would not have mentioned it if we did not have to go there. And he saw we would be swallowed by the sea!"

"Sounds to me that he dreamed all three of you would give yourselves to the sea," Wander said, ambling over to join them.

"His dreams will not cage me!" snarled Danger, his tail lashing back and forth.

"I think the only one caged by his dreams is that poor little fellow," said Wander calmly, glancing at Ofred. "And his dreams don't decide.

They just show him what *you* will decide. But one thing I know is that a raft must go out when the sea goes out. By my reckoning, this tide is near to turning, and if you want to go out with it, the tree-raft will have to be made ready and moved enough so it can float free of the inlet. Unless you want to wait a whole flock of hours until the tide is right again?"

Little Fur took a deep breath and turned back to Danger. "*You* want to be able to change shapes again, and *I* need to rejoin the flow of earth magic. I don't know how this journey can possibly bring us to the earth spirit, but the Sett Owl said it would, just as she said the lemmings would find a new territory."

Danger growled deep in his throat and said, "Even if I come, this shape has a great terror of water. I do not know if I can master it enough to get on the raft."

"Wander is right. If Ofred has dreamed of us on the raft, you will master your fear," said Little Fur.

The moon had set by the time they finished their preparations. Little Fur's cloak was tied to a thick upstanding branch and folded up, ready to be unfolded and tied to another when they wished to catch the wind. She had also tied onto the same branch a number of lengths of coarse twine that Wander had found; he said that if the sea was rough, they might be glad of them. They ate some of the food Wander had found; the rest was pushed into a dry hole at the top of the tree trunk.

A strange soft gourd, as clear as the water that now filled it, was caught in the branches. It smelled bad, as did the white stuff caught in the branches of the tree, but Little Fur was glad they had it, for they would need fresh water. No matter what happened, they must not drink of the great sea, lest its wildness enter them and make them mad. So Brownie had once told her, and so Wander had confirmed.

There was no time for lengthy goodbyes, for the tide had turned. Little Fur stepped onto the trunk and found a place beside her cloak. Ofred climbed into the crook of two branches, followed by Silk and the traveling lemmings. Once Ofred was in place, he closed his eyes, as if, for once, he preferred his dreams to reality.

Now it was Danger's turn. He had been standing atop the outcrop, watching them calmly, but the moment Little Fur looked up at him, a shiver ran over his shining coat. Little Fur could smell the battle raging inside him. Several times he crept forward, whiskers and ears twitching, tail coiling and uncoiling, and then he would shrink back. It seemed he could not force the shape to do something so unnatural. But, paw by paw, Danger won his battle, and at last he clawed his way along the tree trunk and sank into an unhappy crouch.

"Now or never," Ofred whispered as a great wave washed into the inlet, lifting the tree.

"Now!" Little Fur cried.

The wander pushed hard at the trunk with his front paws. The tree dislodged with a great

creaking and scraping of wood. When the water flowed out of the inlet, the tree, with its small band of passengers, was carried out, too.

"I will wait!" Wander shouted. "Come back and tell me the end of the story!" He rose onto his hind legs, looking utterly undoglike as he lifted his hairy paw in farewell.

The tree rotated as each wave met the one behind it. The travelers were forced to cling to their raft to keep from being flung into the water. After a long buffeting period, the waves flattened out. They were already so far from the land that it was no more than a dark smudge against the starlit sky.

Little Fur felt as if she were abandoning all that was certain to journey upon the vast watery riddle that was faith: faith that Gem and the old Sett Owl had been right, faith that Ofred's dreams would bring them to the earth spirit. *And what is faith, truly,* she thought, *but another name for hope?*

Little Fur did not know how the others felt, for they had barely spoken since leaving the shore. Danger slept, claws sunk deep into the dark red wood of the tree trunk. Ofred slept, too, though he cried out often, and each time he did, Little Fur anxiously wondered what he was dreaming.

Little Fur could not sleep. Perhaps it was the ache of moving farther and farther away from Ginger and Crow, or the deeper pain of being cut off from the flow of earth magic—or maybe the heaviness weighing down her spirit came from the weakening of her elf blood. She would have felt lonelier if several of the lemmings had not come to sit on her knees. The lemmings only spoke to her if they had something important to say or if she asked them something directly, but she liked hearing their soft words to one another. Their warm, reverent, sometimes absurd chatter about their adopted master, as they called Ofred, made her smile.

Little Fur gazed down, and one lemming immediately looked up into her eyes. It was Silk, whose eyes shone and whose nose twitched. In that moment Silk looked so like Lim that Little

Fur's own eyes filled with tears. She saw the lemming's eyes widen and fought to control a wave of despair and fear and weariness.

"What is the matter, Healer?" Silk whispered.

"It is only that I am unhappy to be so far from . . . from the land," Little Fur said.

This was true, but it was such a small part of the whole truth that Little Fur wondered if it was a lie. Was it a sign that Little Fur's troll blood was beginning to overpower her elf blood? Yet she did not want to burden the little creature. And if it was a lie, could it be bad if the teller meant only kindness with it? She stroked Silk until the lemming curled back to sleep, and in soothing the lemming, she found that she was soothed herself. She drowsed and then dreamed.

In her dream, she heard the cracked and ancient voice of the old Sett Owl, saying, "All is not as it seems. You must go to the source."

"How can riding on the back of the great sea bring me to the source?" Little Fur asked.

"Under sky, under water, under all that the humans build, is earth," answered the Sett Owl.

"But how are we to get to earth through all this water?" asked Little Fur.

"Only in the deepest green will there be

understanding." The owl suddenly looked straight into Little Fur's eyes. "The wizard understood. She saw what was needed. Do not fail her."

Little Fur puzzled herself awake, for the words of her dream were not all words that the old Sett Owl had spoken in reality. Yet she had the feeling that she had heard some of them before, somewhere else. She opened her eyes and forgot her dream in wonder at the unimaginable bright endlessness of the great sea, heaving and yearning to the horizon on all sides.

Both the moon and the sun were visible, hung at either side of the sky, as if between them they would stop time.

CHAPTER 11
The White Tower

For hours the raft was gentled and nudged along by the shimmering swells. All of the travelers were awake, but still there was almost no talk. It was as if in leaving the land they had lost that which connected them and made talk possible. Whenever Little Fur looked at Danger in the midst of that long, dreamlike day, his eyes were closed but his tail was flickering.

In the afternoon, the dull peace that had lain over her wits began to erode with hunger and thirst. Little Fur got out the food that Wander

had brought them
and poured some of
the water from the
gourd into a hollow
in the tree; then she
called the others to
eat. She hoped that
she was not making a
mistake in rousing
Danger and that his

panther shape would not make him want to eat
some of the lemmings, but he came as quietly as
Ofred to lap at the pool of water. Danger even
refused her offer of food, saying that he felt too
ill. Ofred and the lemmings nibbled at the nuts
and grasses and roots.

In the midst of this strangest of meals, Ofred
suddenly rose up on his hind legs and raised his
arms as if he were about to make a speech.

"Ofred?" Little Fur said, but the lemur was
only stretching. When he subsided, Little Fur
had the mad desire to laugh, but somehow she

knew that if she began, it might be hard to stop.

The sky and sea dimmed to gray, a distant rumble of thunder sounded, and the wind began to blow more briskly, ruffling the sea into low gray peaks edged in a froth of white foam. Little Fur looked up and saw that a monstrous bank of black clouds edged in purple was blotting out half the sky. Lightning flickered from the undersides of the clouds, and the air smelled of rain. They were right in the path of a storm.

"Take shelter! Storm!" Little Fur called to the lemmings as she snatched up a piece of twine and tied it around Ofred's waist.

The lemur blinked at her with wide red eyes and said softly, "The storm will break us."

There was no time for Little Fur to ask Ofred if he had seen this in a dream, for the wind was growing stronger by the second. The waves reared high, the foam at their upper edges torn away into long, wet veils. The tree spun and rocked so that Little Fur could barely keep on her feet, but the widespread branches kept it from rolling over.

Little Fur took another length of twine and crawled to Danger, but he reared up at once and snarled horribly. She struggled back to Ofred, half blinded by the wildly fluttering streamers of her red hair. She wedged herself into the branches alongside the white stuff, which was strangely warm, as if returning her own body heat. No wonder the lemur had pressed himself to it! Cuddling close to him, she shouted out to Danger to join them. He stayed where he was, pressed flat to the trunk, claws plunged deep into the wood.

As the storm closed in on them, lightning cracked and forked overhead, growing brighter until each flash cast a brief light over waves that rose up in black crags. Thunder rumbled overhead. The wind gathered force, and the crags became sheer mountains of darkness marbled with foam that reared up and toppled over.

Little Fur was grateful for Wander's twine, for without it she and Ofred would have been swept away as the waves began to wash over the tree. She feared for Danger, but whenever she glimpsed

him in the flickering light, he was still grimly clinging to the trunk. She could only hope that the lemmings were not drowning in their holes.

Gasping for air in a world turned to water, Little Fur again felt the wildness of the magic in the great sea. In all that wetness, she reminded herself that Ofred had dreamed of land. It was hard to believe in it now—hard to believe in anything but the bellowing storm and the raging sea. Little Fur looked at Ofred, huddled beside her, and saw that his eyes were open, and shining red and wild as a blood moon.

It cannot get worse, Little Fur told herself. *It must end soon.* But it *did* get worse, and it did *not* end. The air became so wet with spray that it was impossible to know where the sea ended and the air began. Ofred curled into a furry ball, and Little Fur could not see Danger at all.

Then, suddenly, it became utterly still and silent.

Little Fur roused herself from her stupor and looked about, still imagining she could hear the howling of the storm. But she was not imagining it, for all around them wind and water roared and churned and heaved. It was as if the two elements were determined to destroy one another or to create some other element altogether.

Only the circle of sea where the tree-raft floated was still, as if they were caged in peace. The water shone, bright silver. Little Fur stood and looked up to see the moon staring down through a hole in the clouds like a cold eye. She shivered and wondered what powerful magic this was, and what it could mean.

"We are in the eye of the storm," Danger said. He was shivering, but his words were calm. He had managed to separate himself from the terror of the panther shape he wore. Indeed, the calmness in his voice appeared to soothe the panther shape. Danger rose and stretched his back into a bow; then he stretched each paw and shook his tail before saying, "The she-human who kept the key to my cage said that there was a storm in me, but that, like all storms, there was a silent center, too. The eye of the storm, she called it."

Little Fur was about to ask how Sly had managed to get the key when she saw that the battered tree was approaching the edge of the circle of calmness. Only then did she understand that if *this* was the center of the storm, then they must pass yet through the other side of it. She glanced in dismay at Danger as he flattened himself to the tree once more. Little Fur barely had time to sit down before the storm snatched them up again.

The roar and violence of the waves felt all the more brutal because of the brief respite. The tree sank, then climbed a gigantic peak of water only to be slammed down under a bigger wave. Little Fur heard the snap of branches. When the lightning flashed again, she saw that the loss of the branches had unbalanced the tree, so that it tilted in the water. Danger was now in a precarious position, clinging to the side of the tree trunk, his eyes slits of fear.

Terrified for him lest more branches should

break, Little Fur loosened the line about her waist until it was long enough to allow her to reach Danger. Then she tied another length of twine to it and began to crawl toward him. As she crept along, she tried to find a pattern in the motion of the water so that she would know when to reach for Danger and tie the line about him. It would not hold his weight, but it might steady him enough to allow him to claw his way up to a safer position.

Again and again waves rushed over the tree trunk, but at last she reached the sodden panther. Even over the wild wet smell of the storm she could smell the sharp reek of his fear. "I am going to tie a line around you," she shouted.

Danger's eyes widened. With a chill, she saw that he was not looking at her, but behind her. Then she saw rising up in his eyes the shadow of a wave, green and monstrous, and she reached out desperately to Danger. She felt his soft wet fur under her fingertips; then a mountain of water slammed down on them. Little Fur felt the roughness of bark under her cheek the moment before she was torn away from the tree and dragged into the churning tumult of the sea. She gasped in a mouthful of water as the line about her waist tightened; then something struck her on the head and she was knocked unconscious.

Little Fur awoke to a cloudless lemon-colored sky and a dazzle of sunlight reflecting off still water. Her nose told her that it was late afternoon. She tried to sit up, only to feel a sharp pain in her middle. She looked down and saw it was from the line around her waist, which was pulled painfully tight. Working at the knots with her stiff fingers, she sat up and found that she was on a floating piece of the white stuff that had been trapped in the branches of the tree.

There was no sign of the tree itself, save for the single thick branch floating close by. It had splintered at the end where it had broken away from the tree, taking her with it. The line about her waist was connected to the branch, and her heart leapt when she saw that her precious cloak was not lost. This reminded her of the green stone. Little Fur put her hand to her neck. It was still there.

There was no sign of Ofred. Little Fur tugged the branch until it was bobbing alongside the white stuff. She untangled her cloak, and there lay Ofred, curled beneath it!

Blinking away tears of relief, Little Fur shook him gently. She whispered his name until he stirred and uncurled himself. Then he picked his way onto the white raft. Settling back on his haunches, Ofred blinked at her with pale red eyes before turning to gaze out at the shimmering sea.

Little Fur thought of Danger and the lemmings. A sharp, dark part of her wanted to hurt Ofred because he had lived and the others had not. After all, had he not dreamed they would all come safe to land? Little Fur knew that the desire to punish came from the growing imbalance between her elf and troll blood—how could she blame the lemur? And in the end, Danger had chosen to follow the lemur's dreams on his own.

"I am thirsty," Ofred said, but their gourd of fresh water was gone.

Little Fur gave Ofred some of the seeds from inside one of the pockets in the hem of her cloak. He nibbled at them stoically. Little Fur looked around at the glittering water and thought how strange it was to be surrounded by wetness and yet unable to drink. They floated for a thirsty while; then Ofred curled back to sleep. Little Fur found she could not do the same. Her mouth was too dry, and her heart hurt too much. She also felt the aching pull that came from being so far away from Ginger and Crow.

At last the sky darkened and stars began to prick through the blackness. The moon had not yet risen, and the sea offered the reflections of the stars so that it looked as if they were floating in the sky. A faint wind began to blow. Little Fur broke two sticks off the larger branch and pushed them very carefully into the white stuff, for their new raft was far less sturdy than the tree had been. She tied up her cloak between the sticks to

catch the wind. She had
no idea where it would
carry them, but it lifted
her spirits to see how the
cloth belled out gently as
they began to move.

The wind bore them
gracefully across the
dark water, until it felt to
Little Fur that the hours
had turned to water and were trickling away
through her fingers before she could drink them.
But they did not come to land. Little Fur eventually lay down beside Ofred. She tried to remember
all that the old Sett Owl and Gem had said, but
it seemed as if she had not seen them for many
years. She thought again of Lim's little golden
pulse of life, which she had failed to hold, and a
coldness touched her.

Little Fur opened her eyes and discovered that
she had slept after all, for now the air about them

was thick with mist. The dampness eased her parched mouth, and when she saw that there were tiny drops in her hair, she ran her fingers lightly over the strands and licked the moisture from them. Then she noticed that there was a little puddle of water where mist had run down the folds of the limp cloak to pool in a depression in the fabric. Whether it was elf magic or simply the way the cloth was made, it held the water safe.

Little Fur shook Ofred until he awoke and made him drink some of the mist-water. Then she drank, too. It was not enough for either of them to properly quench their thirst, and yet it meant they would survive. Little Fur was carefully arranging the cloak to catch more water when she saw that Ofred was haloed in a shimmer of radiance cast by a great shining beam of false light blazing from behind him.

And false light meant humans.

Heart hammering, Little Fur shifted so that she could see past the lemur. She squinted her eyes against the beam of light cutting through the

mist. The light was coming from a high window in a white tower that rose straight up out of the sea like an admonishing finger.

CHAPTER 12
The Deepest Green

The powerful beam of false light arced away, but in a short time it swung back. Little Fur was terrified that the human directing it had seen them, but the light swung away again. This continued to happen until Little Fur's fear ebbed. It was clear that the light was not seeking them out, but following some pattern of its own. They were simply in its path.

Little Fur knew that a human might still become curious about the flashes of white as the light hit the raft, so she untied her cloak and

draped it around herself and Ofred. It was not wide enough to conceal the raft, which worried Little Fur. And a current was carrying them slowly and inexorably toward the white tower.

As they drew nearer to the tower, Little Fur saw that it did not rise up straight out of the sea, as she had first thought, but had been built upon a small, rocky island. This island was ringed by a maze of rocks and other small, stony islands. Little Fur could not help feeling curious about why humans would build a tower in the midst of the great sea. Were they seeking the same mastery over the water that they had achieved over the land? And what was the purpose of the beam of light, playing out its dance over and over upon the misty sea? Unlike the high houses in the city, the tower was not made of unmelting ice, but of smooth stone. It was completely round, with only a door at the base and small windows high up from which shone the beam of false light.

Ofred at last noticed the light. He sat up and gazed at it.

"Did you dream of this?" Little Fur asked him.

"It is the safe place," said Ofred, blinking.

The lemur did not smell of fear, and Little Fur wondered if he understood that false light always meant humans. Ofred turned his head slowly and looked away from the light and the white tower. His gaze was so intent that Little Fur followed it. Something dark was swimming toward them through the mist.

A sleek furred head emerged from the water. "Greetings, Little Fur," came a bright voice. "My name is Trik."

It could only be one of the selkies that Brownie had told her about!

"How do you know my name?" Little Fur asked as the head of another selkie emerged beside the first.

"Who does not know the name of she who stopped the tree burners from killing the seven sacred trees;

175

who journeyed to Underth to save the earth spirit from the tricks of the Troll King; who went to the ice mountains to save her friend?" Trik asked, a teasing note in her voice.

"But *how* do you know of me?" Little Fur asked with as much dignity as she could muster.

Before the selkie could answer, the beam of false light swung back to shine on all of them.

"We must not stay here," Little Fur said urgently. "The human will see us!"

"What human?" asked the other selkie, a male.

"The human that makes the light dance upon the sea," Little Fur said.

"There is no human," answered Trik firmly. "It is only a human device to make the light dance. But there is sweet water ashore, and you smell of thirst. We will bring you to the island, for your raft will break on the reef that surrounds it."

"But how will we get to the island if the raft cannot?" asked Little Fur.

"There are gaps in the reef, but none wide enough for your raft," Trik said.

Little Fur did not want to leave the raft, but the white stuff was beginning to crack and crumble, and it would not bear them for much longer. And she was dreadfully thirsty.

Little Fur helped Ofred into the water, where he began to swim with a good deal of wild-eyed splashing until the two selkies bore him up and carried him smoothly toward the reef. They vanished, and Little Fur's heart sank. But in a short time, the three heads reappeared in the calm water between the reef and the rocky shore of the island. Then Ofred was safely ashore.

By the time the selkies returned for her, Little Fur had tied the cloak about her neck. She slipped into the chill water and at once felt the hungry magic in the waves tugging and nudging at her. The sea magic felt far more powerful than it had by the sandy shore of the mainland. The selkies swam on either side of her, drawing her along far more swiftly and smoothly than she could have swum alone in the rock-studded churn of water. Even so, the wildness of the water was daunting.

"Do not be afraid, Healer, for *this* shape knows well how to swim," the male selkie said soothingly.

Little Fur's mouth fell open, for she recognized his voice. "Danger!" she cried.

"I am," he said, chuckling in a way that must come from this new shape, for Little Fur had never heard him laugh in his panther form. "It may be that my name must be changed," Danger went on, "for it does not fit this shape at all. There is too much laughter and mischievous daring in it. Yet I cannot change my name every time I change my shape."

"What happened?" Little Fur asked incredulously. "I thought the sea had swallowed you!"

"It did," said Danger. "It dragged me deep under the waves. I was beginning to join the world's dream when Trik came to me. She meant just to save me, but when she touched me, I felt the rightness of her shape for that place. I yearned so strongly to be like her that it was so. She was surprised, but no more so than I!"

"So you *didn't* need to go to the earth spirit after all," Little Fur murmured.

Trik bade Little Fur hold her breath at that moment. Then Trik and Danger carried Little Fur down into the fierce green water and through a submerged hole in the reef. They soared back to the surface and Little Fur glided through the calm water to where Ofred waited.

To Little Fur's amazement, there were several lemmings with the lemur, Silk among them.

"However did you get here?" Little Fur marveled.

"The selkies came and found the tree. They pushed it here to the reef, and we swam to this island of the shining light while they went to find you," said Silk. "Now come to the fresh water and food."

Little Fur turned to speak to Danger, but he and Trik were already in the water, diving and splashing. So instead Little Fur followed Ofred, who was picking his way across the water-slicked stones, urged on by the lemmings. Little Fur was very glad to have her feet on solid ground again, though she staggered slightly, as if the ground were tilting. Her heart clenched, for surely this was a sign that the elf part of her was failing. Then she saw that Ofred was staggering, too, and her heart calmed.

"We knew you would come safe to land because the master dreamed it," Silk told Little Fur earnestly when they reached the base of the white tower, where a little feast was laid out. "We foraged in preparation."

There were tiny shellfish and sea grapes, as well as eggs donated by the gulls. Silk explained that the island was home to a great flock of gulls. They had been very happy to see the lemmings and, excited by the prospect of even more company, had flown out to search for Little Fur and Ofred.

"Soon they will return," Silk said as they drank from a spring of icy water. The lemming offered Ofred some of the sea grapes, and then she brought some to Little Fur, adding, "The gulls are eager to meet the one who will enter the maw of the sea."

This news wiped the smile from Little Fur's face.

Another lemming offered her some seeds, explaining that he had harvested them from the great tree that had carried them across the sea.

"But I thought you swam through the reef," Little Fur said, puzzled.

"We did," Silk replied, going on to explain that the tree had been driven onto the rocks and broken. The wind and waves had carried part of it over the rocky reef, and it now lay on the shore of the island. "Would you like to see it?"

Little Fur nodded. Silk and the lemmings guided Little Fur down the other side of the island to a wide, still lagoon protected by the reef. Here, where there was no wild sea to scour it away, was a sandy little beach. Part of the broken tree lay on it, already sinking into the sand. It had lost most of its smaller branches, but there

were still several with tatters of dead leaves and rubbish. Little Fur wondered for the first time in which land the tree had grown, and how it had come to be in the great sea.

"It is lucky it was not swallowed by the maw of the sea," said Silk.

Little Fur looked at her, and a chill ran down her spine. "What do you mean?" she asked.

"Trik said the maw is out there, among the

shoals beyond the reef," Silk said, pointing.

Little Fur could see nothing but the black bar-
rier of the reef. Beyond it was a wild churn of
waves and jagged rocks, but she had no doubt
that whatever the maw of the sea was, it was
there. There was a raucous call overhead, and
she looked up to see a net of gulls descending.
The gulls called out rough greetings and landed,
and the lemmings clustered about them eagerly.
The birds dropped seeds and leaves—and even a
few roots!

"They want us to stay, and they have promised
to feed us," said Silk, who had come to stand
beside Little Fur. "We told them that although
there is good water, we cannot stay where the
earth spirit does not flow."

Ofred had come down to the shore, too. He
was gazing out to sea in the direction that Silk
had pointed to, and he was trembling.

At dusk Little Fur went down to the sandy shore,
for she had seen the selkies in the lagoon. She sat

on a rock and waited until the darker one swam over to her, which he did quickly.

"Will you stay in this shape?" Little Fur asked Danger, as casually as she could.

"I could change now, if I wished," said the shapeshifter, answering the question she had wanted to ask rather than the one she had asked. "After I took this shape, I remembered how to change. Curiosity plus yearning equals change."

"So you will stay this way?" Little Fur asked.

"I will keep this shape until I understand the joy in it," he answered. Then he gave her a shrewd look. "In giving myself to the sea, I found what I sought," he said.

"I thought you would come with me to the earth spirit," Little Fur murmured.

"I thought so, too," Danger replied. Little Fur smelled his pity for her.

"Silk told me the maw of the sea is very near," she said in a low voice.

"It is on the other side of the reef, among the rocks," Danger told her. "Trik showed it to me."

He hesitated. "I do not think you can enter it and live."

"I must go into the mouth of the sea, for that is what Ofred dreamed. If I am to find the earth spirit, I must follow his dreams." Little Fur sighed. "Perhaps the only way for me to rejoin the earth spirit is to join the world's dream."

"I do not think so," Danger said. "For if that were so, you would not have needed to come so far."

That was true, Little Fur reflected, and hope stirred in her. She stood up, suddenly resolute. There was no sense in delay. "How do I get to it?"

"The selkies will take us to the maw of the sea, where we will be swallowed and come to the deepest green," said Ofred, who was coming down to the sand, toward her.

Once again, the selkies brought them through the jagged bite of the reef. By now Ofred was shivering with cold. Little Fur saw that there was another wide lagoon beyond the first. The low-lying sun had turned the water in the lagoon to a milky gold without a fleck of blackness. Although no wave ruffled its surface, there was motion. It was not the wild churn of the waves, but a smooth spiraling of water such as fish and waterbirds make when they dive deep and fast, pulling the water down after them. As they drew closer, Little Fur saw that the spiraling was, in fact, an enormous whirlpool.

The selkies brought Little Fur and Ofred to a rocky outcrop at the edge of the whirlpool. "It is a maelstrom," said Trik with unusual gravity. The sound of the word was deep and compelling and mysterious. "Danger says that you must go into it, but perhaps you will change your mind?"

"It is the way to the deepest green," Ofred said. "Here is the end of all dreams." His eyes blazed red in the fading light.

Little Fur felt the wind of the maelstrom in her hair, felt its voracious hunger in the water. She had no doubt that an end for her lay within it if she surrendered to its call. "Someone told me once that in every ending there is a beginning," she said. Though the words smelled of truth, she could not remember when she had heard them or who had said them. She looked into the shining eyes of the shapeshifter. "Can you take me closer?"

Danger did not answer.

"We cannot go more than a little farther, lest the maelstrom devour us," said Trik.

Little Fur looked at the lemur. "You could choose not to obey your dream, just this once," she said.

"I will go into the maw," said Ofred.

Little Fur drew a deep breath. "We will go together, then. To death, maybe, or to some fate no one has dreamed of."

Ofred and Little Fur entered the water with the selkies again. The pull of the whirlpool was stronger, as if it knew what they had decided. The selkies swam only a short distance; then Trik said, "We will be sucked in if we go any farther."

Little Fur bade the lemur hold on to her neck.

He could swim, of course, but she did not want them to be separated. He climbed from Danger's back onto Little Fur's.

Little Fur had to swim hard to keep them both afloat. She had no breath to say farewell to the selkies, nor was there time—the maelstrom had got hold of them! It pulled them into its slow outer whorl, and Little Fur saw that at the center was a deep green funnel going down into shadow: the maw of the sea.

Little Fur and Ofred circled ever more swiftly as each turn brought them closer to the center. While they were turning on the very edge of the deep green well in the middle of the maelstrom, Little Fur had a sudden memory of climbing down into the misty chasm where the tree guardian lived. Then she and Ofred were drawn over the lip.

Little Fur had thought they would fall into it as into a hole, but the force of the spinning water held them and they turned round and round at a dizzying speed. The tunnel narrowed and darkened as they spiraled down.

Realizing what must happen at the bottom, Little Fur shouted, "Ofred! Hold your breath!" But she did not know if he heard, for all at once they were at the bottom. The force of the envel- oping water was so  great that it nearly tore the lemur from her. Her own terror might have overwhelmed her, but all the trollish stubbornness and strength in her was bent on keeping hold of the lemur. She closed her eyes and had a vision of Crow flying above Gin- ger, who was racing across a sea of bending grass.

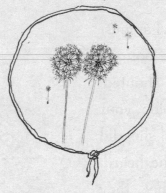

CHAPTER 13

The Source

Little Fur fell, holding her breath until she couldn't anymore. The moment she gave up and breathed was the moment the water was gone. She took in a breath of air and opened her eyes. Little Fur felt a tightness around her neck loosen as Ofred fell to the ground. Little Fur knelt beside the lemur and touched him. He stirred and sat up with a groan.

They were in a tunnel that looked exactly the same in both directions. There was no way to tell where it led, but above them was a great opening, over which flowed the swirling blue-green water of the maelstrom. There was nothing to prevent it from flowing into the tunnel, and so it must be that magic kept it at bay, though Little Fur could not feel magic at all. But how had she passed through the magic then?

"It must be magic keeping the sea out," she said to Ofred companionably. "Though I do not know why it would let us enter."

The lemur said nothing, but he was soaked and shivering.

Little Fur's elf cloak was already dry, and faintly warm about her shoulders. She drew the lemur closer and draped it around him as well, knowing its magic would take the chill from his bones. Thinking of her father's cloak made her check for her mother's stone again. She was relieved to find it where it belonged, around her neck. She thought of the Troll King and felt a hard jab of anger, for was not this perilous journey his fault?

Little Fur stood up, and her troll senses reached

out to feel all the different elements and layers of the surrounding earth. It did not take her long to discover that the tunnel was simply a loop, leading to and from a cavern not far away but deeper down in the earth. She looked at Ofred. "I am going to see where the tunnel leads."

The lemur rose and followed her. Little Fur's senses continued to feel the earth through which they walked. She felt that the tunnel had once been much closer to the surface of the world, for there were traces of land plants in the ground. Not just grass either, but deep roots of great trees. Some unimaginably huge disturbance must have sunk this part of the earth and brought the sea down on it.

Little Fur thought of the sea that had flooded the valley where her father and her mother had been held captive in the she-wizard's castle. She wondered if the same flood that had marked the end of the age of magic had covered the hole under the sea, and whose magic had stopped it up. No one knew where Little Fur's mother had gone after her father had cracked open the earth to save her, but Little Fur was sure that her mother would have returned to her kin—for where else should she go? And she would have been welcomed, for not only was she a troll, she was a princess. Little Fur knew this because the green stone her mother had possessed was bestowed only upon trolls of royal blood.

But something had clearly gone wrong. Why else would Little Fur have been left as a babe in the roots of the eldest in the grove of the Old Ones, with only her mother's stone around her neck and her father's cloak wrapped about her? She had questioned the ancient trees, but they said only that one morning, when the sun opened its eye, she had been cradled in the roots of the eldest of them.

Little Fur shivered and saw a mist of green light ahead. She and Ofred emerged from the tunnel into what seemed to be an immense cavern, such as those in which the troll city of Underth was built. It was difficult to see what lay within the cavern because of the green mist, but Little Fur could make out a path winding down toward several enormous rock formations. As they drew closer, Little Fur saw that the humped shapes were natural formations that had been carved and given graceful doors and windows. They passed by deserted dwelling after deserted dwelling, until Little Fur understood that what they were in had once been a great city.

Utterly astonished, Little Fur wondered what sort of creatures had built the city, for it was far too ancient to be a human settlement. She had only to touch a wall to know that the stone had been shaped when the eldest of the seven great singing trees was planted, which meant it must be a city from the age of magic!

Little Fur went on, marveling at how the builders of the city had sculpted stone in a way that revealed all of its hidden beauty. Humans built on the earth and smothered it, but here every dwelling was shaped to revere the stone from which it was fashioned! Some of the dwellings

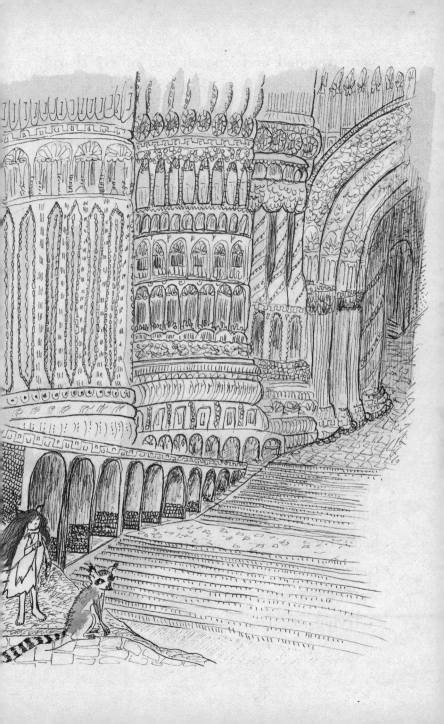

were rounded and smooth and others sharply faceted, but all took their form from the stone.

Little Fur and Ofred passed sets of stairs that rose in dizzying spirals until they dissolved in green light. Little Fur's troll senses told her that the steps went right up to the roof of the cavern and had once led to open air, but now they were blocked by earth. These, too, must have been closed by magic. Little Fur wondered if this had perhaps been a city of wizards.

Suddenly she stopped, for the path they were following had brought them by a building so very like the round house where Lim had died that Little Fur could not doubt that the same kind of creature had made it. Was it possible that humans could have uprooted the round house and carried it to their city? Certainly some humans were almost as curious as cats. And being human, they would not think to leave the round house where it was, for they always wanted to possess things that interested them.

Trying to puzzle things out, Little Fur went

closer. She gasped when she saw that runes had been carved into the side of the round house. They were *troll* runes such as she had seen in ruined tunnels above Underth, but these were far more beautifully and carefully formed. This had been a city of trolls!

The ends of Little Fur's furled ears tingled. No story she had ever heard had spoken of trolls capable of building like *this*. Other creatures left over from the age of magic sometimes said that trolls belonged to an earlier age of the world. Was it possible that there had been an age of trolls in which they had been great workers of stone and earth and makers of runes? But if so, why did no creature know of it? And what had happened to turn trolls into what they had become?

The only thing Little Fur could think of was

that there had been two kinds of troll, and that the rune-makers had been overcome by the more savage kind. Indeed, there might have been many kinds of troll. She thought of the trolls she had seen in Underth, who had seemed to be slaves to the others there. Perhaps the slaves were the remnants of the rune-makers? Little Fur's heart beat fast at the thought that her mother might have been just such a rune-maker. Yet that did not make sense, for how could a troll princess become a rune-maker, let alone a slave?

Ofred laid his soft black paw on her arm and Little Fur started, for she had completely forgotten him in her fascination with the city.

"This was built by trolls," she told him, running her fingers over the runes and letting her troll senses feel them out. She could almost grasp their meaning, but even though her troll blood was much stronger than it had been before, she could not quite manage it.

"Once my elf blood is gone, I will be able to read the runes," she murmured. Then she staggered in horror at the ease with which she had uttered this terrible thought. It showed how near her elf blood was to being quenched. "Stop!" she cried, shouting the words so that the cavern threw them back at her in a hundred broken echoes.

Ofred plucked at her arm.

"What is it?" Little Fur snapped.

"There is something under us," said Ofred, his red eyes strange in all that greenness. "I can feel it."

Little Fur dropped to her knees. Was it the earth spirit? She pressed her palms to the earth, her heart thundering. She was shocked to find not the earth spirit but another harling!

"Greetings, Troll," the harling boomed. The voice was female. "It has been long since one of your kind walked here." Ofred gave a whimper of surprise.

"What . . . what happened to the trolls who lived here?" Little Fur asked.

"There was a war, and they were driven out," said the harling.

"A war! But who made war on the trolls?" asked Little Fur.

"Elves," the harling answered. "They desired an end to stone magic, and they believed that the working of magic should be left to their kind and to wizards."

Little Fur licked her lips. "What *is* stone magic?"

"It is strange that a troll knows nothing of the making of stones that can hold magic, for it was once a great art among trollkind," murmured the harling.

"*Trolls* worked magic?" Little Fur asked, trembling with astonishment.

"Your kind could not work pure magic like elves and wizards," said the harling. "But they shaped trollstone to draw in a tiny amount of pure magic. Then they could use their power over earth and stone to make use of it."

Little Fur felt as if she had been hit on the head. The Sett Owl had said her stone was empty, even though the Troll King had thought it full. And she had wondered what could possibly fill a stone. Now she knew—magic!

Little Fur felt the harling move closer to the surface, though not close enough to crack the earth between them. The earth dragon moved as easily and smoothly as if she were swimming, which meant the flow of earth magic was very powerful here. Little Fur closed her fingers over her green stone.

"What is this?" the harling said. Little Fur felt the earth dragon's curiosity stirring like a great slow underground river. "You are not wholly troll. There is elf blood in you, though it is very thin. How can this be?"

"My mother was a troll and my father was an elf," said Little Fur.

To Little Fur's surprise, the harling began to laugh. The sound was like a shower of rocks falling down a deep well. "The child of an elf and a troll! What strange riddle is this?"

Little Fur was surprised to hear the harling speak of her birth as a riddle, but it also reminded her of her quest. "I have come here to find the earth spirit," she said. "Do you know where it is?"

Little Fur sensed that the earth dragon had sobered. "You must follow the troll path to the deepest green," she said.

"Thank you," said Little Fur. She was about to rise when she remembered the harling under the round house. She told this harling of him. "Perhaps you can go and bring him here?" she suggested.

"That is not possible," replied the she-harling gravely. "There are three of us who remain near the once-great city of Trollesund, where earth magic is potent enough to let us move easily through the earth. But to go to the surface of the world from this deep place would take many eons, for the closer we came, the more slowly we would move."

"Then I will tell the harling to come to you when I go back to the human city," said Little Fur.

"Tell him that he will be welcome among us," said the harling.

Little Fur and Ofred continued through that vast dead city. They went along an avenue of shaped stones such as humans made, but these were shaped into trolls—such trolls as Little Fur had never seen before. They were tall and slender. Their faces were wise and kindly and noble, so Little Fur understood that these were great trolls honored by the other trolls who had dwelt in this city. There was no question, seeing those carved faces, that there had once been a high age of trolls. Anger stirred in Little Fur's troll blood that such a city as this had fallen because elves and wizards had wanted to keep the use of magic for themselves.

Little Fur felt Ofred's eyes on her. She took a deep breath and forced herself to be calm. Her temper might be enough to completely smother what remained of her elf blood! Little Fur forced her mind away from the past and asked the lemur as calmly as she could if he had dreamed of the city.

But he would not, or could not, answer.

At long last, the path wove out of the city and dropped into a deep fold in the earth. The glow of green light there was stronger than ever, but Little Fur could not help glancing back and taking one long, hungry look at the wondrous city. "Trollesund," she said reverently, telling herself that if she could not find the earth spirit in time, she would come back. And she would read the runes to learn about that lost age in which trolls had made this place.

The path became a set of steep steps. Down and down they went. The panels carved on the stone walls on either side showed trolls creating the city through which they had passed. Little Fur saw not just elder trolls with wise and wizened faces, but young, strong troll men and women laboring at their building. Their bodies were well formed and straight-backed, and their expressions were eager and full of joy. Other panels showed troll families dancing around fires, making cloth and metal, and playing strange instruments.

Little Fur found some mushrooms growing thickly on the wall. She and the lemur ate them so greedily that they were forced to sit awhile before they could go on. It got colder the deeper they went, so they stopped to huddle in the warmth of the elf cloak until the lemur's teeth ceased to chatter. Then on they went again.

Little Fur wondered if they would *ever* come to the deepest green. Then the stone and the steps changed to become green like her mother's stone. *Trollstone,* she thought. Her heart began to beat harder, for now she could hear something.

It began as a faint whisper, but little by little, it grew until she realized it was the sound of water. Sniffing, Little Fur could tell it was not salten water but water of the earth.

At last the steps brought them to the open door

of a small chamber. The green light coming from it was so thick that at first Little Fur could see nothing else. Then she saw that there was a well in the middle of the cavern. Its sides were almost as high as her head and heavily carved in runes, row upon row of them, carefully formed and full of mysterious knowledge. This well was far older than the city above and had come from some other place altogether.

Little Fur looked at the lemur. "Is *this* what you dreamed, Ofred?"

Ofred said nothing, but his eyes blazed red with a strange mixture of hope and fear.

Little Fur spoke his name—"Ofred"—but he seemed not to hear. Then she realized he was not listening to her, but to a soft murmurous rushing sound coming from the well of carved green stone.

There were more stone steps leading up the side of the well. Little Fur mounted them and peered down. She was dimly aware of the lemur's leaping up onto the rim to look in, too. Then she forgot about Ofred and the runes and her own plight—for here was a swirling of something that was neither green mist nor green water nor green light, but somehow all these things.

Welcome, Little Fur, said a voice. It rose as much from the chamber and the stones of the well as from whatever strange substance filled it.

Little Fur shivered from head to toe. It was the voice she had heard often before, yet never so clearly and strongly as this. "You are the earth spirit," she whispered.

I am, said the voice.

"How can I hear you when I cannot feel you?" Little Fur asked, trembling at the power that threaded through the voice.

Because of the trollstone, the voice answered.

Little Fur took a deep, shaky breath and asked what she had come so far to ask: "Earth spirit, can you restore me to the flow of earth magic?"

I cannot, said the earth spirit.

The words were a blow to her heart. "Why?" Little Fur cried. She found that tears were streaming down her cheeks. "I did nothing wrong. It was only chance and accidental malice that severed me from you!"

It was not the greeps who cut you off from the flow of earth magic, Little Fur, said the earth spirit gently, and there was compassion in its voice now.

"No? But then . . . who?" asked Little Fur.

I, said the earth spirit. *It was I who severed you from the flow.*

CHAPTER 14

Stone Magic

Little Fur thought of the tiny golden pulse of Lim's life, which had slipped so easily through her fingers. The pain that lay like a stone in her chest grew.

"It is because of Lim, isn't it?" she asked the earth spirit. "It is because I failed to heal him."

The earth spirit laughed.

Little Fur was so surprised that it took a moment for her to hear the kindness and sorrow in the laughter.

Oh, my dearest Little Fur, said the earth spirit. *My*

small brave champion in whom goodness and sweetness and courage meet with a humility that humbles me. Oh, what a thing you are to have been made out of so much hatred and pain and fear.

"I don't understand," said Little Fur, her voice tiny. "If you say such things and mean them, why did you cut me off from the flow of magic?"

Because it was the only way to bring you here, said the earth spirit.

"You were summoning me?"

I needed you to come to me here because only here, where I am strongest, can I tell you clearly what happened to the last age. And it must be told lest the same fate befall this age, said the earth spirit.

"But it is nature for all creatures and all ages to end," Little Fur said. Then she blushed at having spoken in such a way to one who must know all things better than she.

The earth spirit answered, *That is true, but the last age ended eons too soon, because of the great harm that was done which caused it to sicken and die. That* harm has leaked into this age, so that it, too, will hasten to its end.

"The Sett Owl told me I needed to understand," Little Fur murmured.

It would take an age to tell the story of an age, said the earth spirit. *Nor is it all known to me, for I was wild magic before I became the earth spirit — wild magic, as powerful and unaware as that blind tempest of power that flows through the great sea. All I know of the age before this one was gifted to me. Indeed, it was that gifting that formed me. Therefore know this: In the beginning of the age of elves and wizards, trollkind was not degenerate and brutish. Trolls were makers of music and runes, and lovers of beauty. You have seen it yourself, for you have passed through Trollesund, the last and greatest of the troll cities. The last king of Trollesund was Somber. In his keeping was the greatest source of what trolls call trollstone. In shaping it, trolls found a way to draw the wild magic of the earth into the stone, and in that form, they could work magic.*

Little Fur gripped the stone around her neck.

"The Troll King of Underth tried to steal this stone," she said.

Because he does not understand the nature of stone magic. He knows only memories of memories. There is no magic in the stone now. Indeed, there is no troll left who understands the art of stone magic. But even if there were a troll who did know it and who could come to this deep, lost place, earth magic is no longer wild and cannot be drawn like water from a well.

Little Fur touched the stone well in wonder.

This well serves to draw magic near, but it is not made to hold it, said the earth spirit. *Such wells were made wherever there was trollstone in the earth, and a troll would come to one only with the blessing of the king and his wise counsel, in order to shape a single precious stone. It was a thing all trolls did when they came of age, and did once only, for there was only a small amount of trollstone in the world, and most of it was here.*

"So it was not just troll kings and queens who had the stones?" Little Fur asked.

Not in the golden days when stone magic was an art and the trolls were wise and careful, but in the end, the trolls who fled the cities were bidden to give up their stones so that the king could defend them. Since then, only kings and their blood kin have had trollstones.

Again Little Fur looked down at the stone hanging from her neck and said, "My mother's stone is empty."

The earth spirit went on with its story: *Elves and wizards did not need to shape stones, for they drew wild magic from all things, and there was no limit to what they could take. Wizards limited themselves, for they had the gift of foresight. They warned elfkind to go carefully, but the elf kings were proud and clever and bade the wizards mind their own long, slow affairs. They thought wizards dull and tedious, but they despised the trolls who toiled in the earth. In the end, the elves destroyed the wells and buried all the trollstone deep under the earth. Troll city after troll city fell, and each of the deepest greens was destroyed until there was only this last city and this last well. Then it fell, too, and the elves used spells to seal the entries and made the very oceans to close over it.*

Little Fur was appalled. "I did not know elves were bad."

They were not all bad, but capable of badness, as is every creature who can think and choose what to do. The elves believed that they were the natural rulers of their age, and as such, none but they should work magic. But the trolls' working of slow, careful stone magic was one of the things that balanced the age, so once that working ended, the age began to fail.

"But why did the trolls become the way they are since then?" Little Fur asked. "Was it because they had no more magic?"

What happened to them was no more than what happens to any kind that is driven from tradition and custom and hearth by war. They fled and hid, and those who survived were those who were strong and angry. They fought the elves in savage raids, and the more brutal the trolls were, the more brutal they became. Not all were so. Some counseled gentleness and a seeking of new

214

trollstone deposits using the small hoard of filled stones
that had been carried from the sacked cities. But those
voices were not heeded.

"So the elves truly made the trolls what they are," Little Fur said, unable to believe it.

The elves destroyed a great civilization out of pride and conceit, said the earth spirit. *But in doing so, they also destroyed themselves.*

"But you said wizards could see the future," Little Fur said. "Why didn't they warn the elves?"

They tried, but the elves would hear no one's counsel, answered the earth spirit. *Only one wizard used all of her art to see into the age that would come next. It was a very great working, and she saw only a few glimpses of the possible futures that might come. All were short, ruinous ages that would infect the next and the next age, so that each age would become shorter and more chaotic. All save one future, which would result from the birth of a youngling of both troll and elf blood. Only in that future might the damage done in the age of high magic be healed.*

Little Fur's head spun, for it was clear that she

herself was that youngling in whom elf and troll blood were mingled: here at last was the answer to the riddle of her own birth! The she-wizard who had held her parents captive had contrived her birth not to use her in some fearsome spell, but to save the next age! That was what the old Sett Owl had meant when she had said that Little Fur must not fail the wizard!

"But I do not know how to heal an age!" Little Fur cried, frightened that so much should rest upon her shoulders. "I could not even heal Lim."

He was already half given to the world's dream, said the earth spirit. *There was a sickness in his blood that no healer could mend. Yet I held it off, for I saw a glimpse of what would come in that which you called the round house, which was once the peace house of a troll village. I saw that the small lemming would save your life and perish from the effort. But I stayed his dying until you touched him and tried to heal him, for I knew this was the way to sever you from the flow.*

"I do not understand," said Little Fur.

I knew that no creature had ever joined the world's dream while you cared for it, and that if it did, you would be shaken. I knew that if, in that moment, I withheld the flow, you would believe you had been severed from it.

"But I *was* severed!" Little Fur said. "I *am*!"

You were severed, but all you needed to do was to will yourself back into the flow, as you would have tried to do had the lemming not died. But because of that death, you accepted that you had been cut off from the flow as if it were a punishment. Because cut off from the flow, you saw death as evil rather than natural.

Little Fur took a shuddering breath and reached down into herself, seeking the part of her that communed with the Old Ones. She imagined the sweetness of hearing their whispering, and then she imagined reaching down through their roots into the earth.

NO! The voice of the earth spirit was urgent and full of command.

Frightened, Little Fur ceased striving. "Why not?"

If you rejoin the flow here, so close to me, I would draw

you in even as I draw the flow in, said the earth spirit. *That is why you had to come here severed from the flow. You must wait to reach out until you return to the surface of the world.*

"You would hurt me?" asked Little Fur, shaken.

Again the earth spirit laughed, but now there was great sorrow and yearning in the sound. *I love you more than you can know. If you entered the flow, I could not help but summon you to me.*

"What would you have me do?" Little Fur asked.

No more than that which you have always done, Healer, answered the earth spirit. *You must heal trollkind and bring it to the flow of magic.*

"Heal trollkind?" cried Little Fur, aghast. "I am just—"

A true healer, as the she-wizard foresaw, said the earth spirit with finality and pride.

"I can heal wounds and hurts and sicknesses of the body, but you are talking of something else," protested Little Fur.

I speak of the spirit, that which you have always tended even as you tended the physical hurts of any beast. The spirit of trollkind must be opened to the flow of earth magic.

"How?" Little Fur asked.

I do not know, said the earth spirit. *But the she-wizard foresaw that you would find a way. I had only to bring you here for you to bring balance to this age, so that it should last long and all the trolls and elves and humans and beasts and birds and others that inhabit it can have time to Become.*

"To become?" Little Fur echoed. "To become what?"

To Become all that they can become. I do not know what they can become. That is for each to discover.

"How do you know so much and not know that?"

What I know of the she-wizard and of the fall of trollkind was told to me by the only other who has come here since the city fell—a troll princess. She was heavy with child and fleeing the outrage of her own kindred, for the father of her child was an elf.

"Ardent." Little Fur breathed the name of her father.

Yes, said the earth spirit. *That was the name the troll princess whispered as she slept. Love and sorrow were in that name. He cracked open the earth with a mighty spell that was all that remained of his power, and by pure chance it was that spell which opened a path to the lost city of Trollesund.*

"My mother came to Trollesund?" Little Fur whispered.

Not at once, answered the earth spirit. *First she went to her kindred, but when they learned what sort of child she carried, she realized they would slay it. So she fled again, stealing from her uncle, who was king, the last two full trollstones. The king sent his armies after her, but she came upon the way to this place, drawn by traces of Ardent. She used the magic in the stone you wear about your neck to close the earth behind her. At Trollesund she bore you, and she dwelt there for some time, but you were part elf and she knew that you would need sunlight and green and growing things.*

Then, one day, she came here. You were tiny and she

carried you swaddled upon her back. She was looking for mushrooms when she stumbled upon the steps to this chamber.

Little Fur looked around in wonder. "My mother was *here*?"

She took you into her arms and sat where you now stand. She had learned enough during her time in the city to know that she had found the last well of wild magic. The art of making stone magic was unknown to her, so she tried to command the trollstone to show her how, but that could not be done. She asked the stone to tell her how to save you. Only then did the stone show her that you lived only because you were close to a rich source of earth magic. If you went away from it, you would die. But if you did not get to sunlight and fresh air, the elf part of you would sicken. She was horrified, for this was a riddle that seemed to have no answer. At last, the stone told her that the answer lay in the well of wild magic, but that it would cost all that she possessed.

"What did that mean?" Little Fur asked.

The troll princess believed it meant that she must cast herself into the well.

221

"No!" Little Fur cried, as if she saw her mother before her, poised to leap.

I do not know what the stone magic vision meant, but to do what she believed she must do was dreadfully hard for the troll princess. Not because she feared death, but because she had to abandon you. She would have to trust the stone magic that told her you would be safe.

Little Fur could not imagine how her mother must have felt, sitting and gazing into the mysterious swirl inside the well, with such a terrible choice to make. Then she realized that her mother had not been alone here. She had the baby in her arms.

Me, thought Little Fur with a shiver of her heart. "*I* was in her arms," she said.

Yes, said the earth spirit. *She sat looking at you for a very long time; then at last she wrapped you up in the cloak she wore and hung the stone she had used around your neck. As she cast herself into the well, she touched the stone and willed you to the safest place in all the wide world for one such as you. And so you went deep into a forest of singing trees.*

Little Fur drew in a shuddering breath. So *that* was how she had come to be in the grove of the Old Ones with only her father's cloak and her mother's green stone. "She died for me," said Little Fur softly. "Both of them died because of me."

It might also be said that they had a love worthy of a thousand songs because of you, Little Fur. Never would they have met if the she-wizard had not foreseen the world's need for a child in whom elf and troll bloods were mingled. The troll princess hated the she-wizard, as did Ardent, because they had not understood her purposes. The she-wizard might have explained, but wizards are mysterious, and in the end they might not have believed her. Nor could the she-wizard have done what she did in any other way, given the hatred between elfkind and trollkind. Neither Ardent nor the troll princess would have agreed to the match. And even if they could have been made to see the need, any child they made would have been born of duty. But you are the child of love, and nothing is more powerful or precious than that. It made you, and in the end it made me.

"You?" Little Fur was startled.

Your mother gave her whole life, and so worked a great shaping. She bound a great mass of magic not to stone, but to itself, and so what had been elemental power Became the earth spirit, who could think and feel and choose. And so the flow of earth magic through all things became infused with your mother's love for you. All at once it, or I, was filled with the desire to keep you safe. And as I grew and learned and continued to Become, I understood that to love and nourish you properly, I must love and nourish the world and the age in which you live.

"It was because of my mother that you know about the last age failing and hurting this age?" Little Fur asked.

She learned much in her captivity and afterward, and all that she knew she gave to me when she gave herself. And as I continued to Become, I realized that I must risk what I loved in order to save the age in which you live. It was you who taught me that, for time and time again you risked yourself for me. And so I turned my will to troll-kind, who had closed themselves to me, for I knew they must be drawn back into balance. Yet no troll would open him- or herself to me. The earth spirit fell silent.

Little Fur waited. Finally, the earth spirit said, *Now you must leave this place.*

"Leave?" Little Fur said, bewildered. "But you haven't told me what to do. I don't know how to help the trolls. They will not listen if I beg them to open themselves to you. And besides, I don't know how to leave, because I don't know how we got here."

The maelstrom brought you to an old tunnel that leads to the surface. It is not closed by elf magic, but by the stone magic of King Somber. Because of that, I was able to make it let you pass through without allowing the sea to come in, said the earth spirit.

"But I can't go back that way, can I?" Little Fur asked.

No, said the earth spirit. *You must use stone magic.*

Little Fur looked at the trollstone hung around her neck. "But it is empty. Unless it can be refilled?"

It cannot, said the earth spirit. *But by the wall is the bag your mother carried to this place long ago. In it is the second stone she took from the king. Indeed, it is the last full trollstone in this age. You can use that and return to the surface of the world safely.*

Little Fur looked at Ofred. "I must take the lemur back with me."

You need only hold him when you will yourself away and he will be drawn with you. If he wills it, too.

"Of course he wills it!" said Little Fur, but when she looked at Ofred, he was gazing into the well, as he had been doing all through their long talk. "Ofred?" she said uncertainly.

"In the well is the end of dreams," said Ofred.

As you dreamed, said the earth spirit to him. *Will you gift yourself to me or go with Little Fur?*

There was another long silence. At last Ofred stirred and sighed. "I want to go into the well, but the lemmings are waiting for me to return."

By your dreams they will grow and Become, if you return to them, said the earth spirit.

Again Ofred sighed. "I will go with the Healer." He looked wistfully into the well. "I did not dream that I would choose this."

There are dreams and then there is choosing, said the earth spirit. *Healer, it is time to get the last stone.*

Near the wall Little Fur found the remnant of an ancient bag. Among its dusty fragments, she found a comb and spoon of yellow stone. Then she found the trollstone, clasped in tiny silver claws at the end of a blackened silver chain. She caught the chain in her fingers, and at once the stone pulsed with life. Little Fur felt the power singing in her fingers and saw a deep glow in the stone's depth.

Do not touch it until you are ready, said the earth spirit swiftly, *for it calls to me and I must fight to keep the flow from drawing the wild magic to me, and you with it.*

"What must I do?" asked Little Fur, now holding the stone by its chain.

Hold the lemur and fill your mind with the wish to go to the surface of the world. Then touch the stone.

Little Fur climbed down the steps and reached for the lemur. After a long moment, he took her outstretched hand.

"Goodbye," Little Fur told the earth spirit, looking into the well. But in her heart she thought, *Goodbye, Mother.*

Goodbye, my daughter, said the earth spirit.

Little Fur touched the green stone in her pocket. She filled her mind with an image of the little stony island where the lemmings awaited Ofred. For an instant, she thought she saw a troll woman reach out from the well to her, smiling.

CHAPTER 15
The Gift

It happened in the blink of an eye. One minute they were on the edge of the well in the deepest green, and the next they were standing in the cool air on the island shore. It was early morning, with one or two stars dimming in the pale sky.

This is how it must have happened when I was a baby, Little Fur thought. *My mother leaped into the well and willed me to the Old Ones, and just like that, I was there.*

Little Fur looked down at Ofred, who was

gazing at the horizon, where the sun was just opening its eye.

"I thought I would not see it again," he murmured. "It is more beautiful than I remember."

Little Fur thought he sounded different, less tormented and frightened but older and sadder. Perhaps that was what Becoming meant: to grow and change; to understand more.

Little Fur felt a throb of sorrow for the old Sett Owl. Yet how could she feel sad when the old owl had been so weary and worn and had longed and yearned to join the world's dream? It was the still magic that had kept her alive, just as the earth spirit had kept Lim alive beyond his time. Sometimes Little Fur had wondered why the still magic needed a Sett Owl, but now she thought she understood. The Sett Owl had done for the still magic what her mother had done for earth magic. She had shaped pure power and had given it purpose and will. Now Gem would serve it in the same way. Had she not heard the still magic calling to her? Had she not said it needed her? As for the old Sett Owl, she had died, but there was no reason for sadness, because she had Become all that she could be.

"I am still Becoming," Little Fur said softly to herself.

She heard a cry of delight and saw several lemmings running toward Ofred. In a moment they were all around him, grooming his fur and crooning lovingly to him. Ofred looked at Little Fur, and then at the lemmings. For the first time, he seemed to see them properly. After a long moment, he reached out to touch Silk awkwardly with his little black paw. She ran into his lap and began to talk softly to him, and a moment later, more lemmings were on his lap as well.

Little Fur heard a cheerful bark of greeting and turned to see a gleaming dark head cleaving through the water in the still lagoon. She thought it was Danger, but when it was close, she saw that it was Trik.

"Where is Danger?" Little Fur asked.

The seal gave a soft chuckle. "He is too big now to come here, for he has changed again. If you would speak with him, you must let me bring you through the reef."

The air was rent by a long, haunting call.

"He calls to you," said Trik. "Will you come? He will carry all of you back to the mainland."

Little Fur stared in wonder as a giant gray creature surfaced beyond the jagged rocks. From its head plumed a great spout of water that was carried away in rainbow veils by the wind. The creature was so big that Little Fur thought that she, Ofred and the lemmings could easily fit on its back—though it might be a damp journey! Little Fur turned back to Trik. "But how did he know we were returning?"

"The flow of earth magic told the lemmings, and they told us," answered Trik.

Little Fur frowned. "But earth magic does not flow here."

"It flows," said Silk. "It did not flow and then it began to flow, and in it we saw a picture of you and the master returning. It was a sign and a blessing on this island." There was a murmur of approval from the other lemmings.

Little Fur looked into their fervent faces, and a picture came into her mind of the seeds that they had foraged from the tree. Was it possible one or more of them had fallen as the lemmings carried them over the island, and had begun to germinate? But what a strange chance that a dead tree would wash up on this barren shore bearing seeds just in time to let the earth spirit speak to the lemmings.

Little Fur was about to will herself into the flow when she realized that she might still be too dangerously close to the earth spirit. Better to wait until she had reached the mainland. Little

Fur turned to Ofred and suggested that Trik could take her to Danger and then return for him and the lemmings.

Ofred shook his head. "No," he said. "The lemmings believe this to be the strange and wondrous territory promised them. They wish to stay here, and I will stay with them."

"Are you sure?" Little Fur asked him.

"I am sure of nothing," he said. "Farewell, Healer."

Little Fur gathered the lemur into her arms and held him close. For the first time, he held her, too. Then he let her go and she bade Silk and the other lemmings a lengthy goodbye. Little Fur hesitated to leave them, realizing that they had come so far together and had endured so much that it was hard to imagine going anywhere without them. But the lemmings had decided to stay, and she must return to the mainland.

"I will ask the gulls for news of you," she said to them at last.

"We will send them, and when they return,

they will bring us news of you and the others," said Silk.

The lemmings all nodded, and then they flattened themselves to the ground.

"Goodbye," Little Fur finally said. "I will miss you." She slipped into the water, and Trik brought her through the reef to the enormous creature that Danger had become.

"Little Fur," he sang gently.

"I did not know there were such enormous beasts in the sea," Little Fur shouted.

"I was searching for you when I came upon a

vast animal that smelled of wisdom and patience. I felt these things would be needed to find you. But, Little Fur, though the wisdom in this shape is deeper than the ocean and the patience in it is as wide as time itself, the true beauty of this shape is in its compassion and its gentleness. In such a size, to find such softness! I must understand it."

Little Fur almost envied the shapeshifter his gift.

Danger sank until only a little of his immense form rose above the waves, like a small island, so that Little Fur could scramble onto his back. He rose up again, lifting her high above the water.

Little Fur turned to wave to Ofred and the lemmings. Then Danger began to move at a pace that seemed very slow and stately until she saw how swiftly they left the island and its white tower behind. Trik swam with them for several hours before turning back, but only after exacting a promise from Danger that he would visit her soon.

"How long will it take to reach our land?" Little Fur asked Danger after a time.

"Through most of the night, if there are no storms," he said calmly. After a pause, he said, with some of his old curiosity, "Tell me what happened at the bottom of the maelstrom."

Little Fur told him only that she had found the earth spirit and would be able to rejoin the flow of earth magic as soon as she reached the mainland. The rest was too painful and tangled with sorrows to speak of yet. She wore both stones about her neck now, for there was no risk of the earth spirit drawing her into itself when she was not touching earth.

As the long, serene day wore on, Little Fur thought of many things, and especially of all that the earth spirit had told her. Mostly, she thought of trollkind and wondered how she could convince the trolls to open themselves to earth magic. Perhaps she could use the troll Sly and Danger had captured, though it would be better by far if she could convince the Troll King. If he opened himself to the flow of earth magic, the rest would follow. And once earth magic flowed through them, they would begin to grow and Become whatever it was they ought to have Become in the last age, if the elves had not prevented them from making stone magic.

Unfortunately, she could think of no way to convince the Troll King. Even if she used the magic that remained in the stone to take herself directly to him, he would probably kill her. She turned the riddle over and over in her mind, but could find no answer as the hours of day gave way to dusk, and then to the star-dappled night.

At last, in the silver-gray light before dawn, Little Fur saw a black speck flying like an arrow toward her.

"Little Fur! Little Fur!" screeched Crow, circling overhead. "What are you doing on this big fishiness?"

Little Fur laughed for sheer joy at hearing his dear loud voice, and she shouted for him to land. He refused, exclaiming that Crows were the

favorite food of such vast unnatural creatures as she was riding.

"It is Danger!" Little Fur cried. "He has learned to change his shape again! Come down!"

After some fluttering and flapping and several cries of "Nevermore!" Crow landed on Danger and hopped hastily onto her lap. Little Fur stroked his lustrous black feathers and kissed his head. She told him what a brave, marvelous, clever bird he was, until he was so full of pride that, for the first time in his life, he was silent. Only then did the link they shared with Ginger tell her that the gray cat was also near.

"Ginger?" Little Fur said.

"Ginger riding in the belly of the road serpent," Crow said. "He and some others. They wait on the shorefulness. We came because Gem saw that the mouth of the sea would swallowing you, but that you would returning, with the knowing of how to rejoining the flow of earth magic."

"I do know," said Little Fur, wondering whom he meant when he said "some others." Before she could ask, the sun opened its eye and the sea shone and glimmered. In the distance, Little Fur saw land.

It was not long before they were close enough for her to see the sandy white shore and the black rocks that Ofred and Danger had sat on, waiting for the mysterious gift from the sea. Little Fur could see the shaggy wander sitting on the shore with a little cluster of lemmings around him. As she waved, a net of gulls rose into the sky to weave a pattern of welcome and curiosity. Crow gave a loud caw and flapped up to join them. She looked eagerly for Ginger's gray form, but could not see him.

"Now you must swim, for the land is calling to the sea. If I go nearer, I will be drawn up on the beach, which would be dangerous for this shape," said Danger.

Little Fur was not afraid. To return to land was far easier than sailing away from it. Besides, the land was calling the sea and the sea was surrendering, flowing in and in. She slid off Danger's back into the salten water. "Goodbye, Danger. And thank you!" Little Fur called to the huge beast.

"Tell Sly that I will visit her when I take a shape that can walk on the land again," he sang.

Little Fur promised she would. Then she ceased resisting the waves and let them carry her to land, until she felt the sand under her feet. She staggered a little as the water fell back; then Ginger and Sorrow were on either side of her, urging her to lean on them. When they were on dry sand, she hugged one and then the other and then the first again, laughing and crying in her joy at seeing them.

"What happened to Nobody?" Little Fur asked Sorrow.

"The human is caring for her," said the fox, a flicker of gold in his green eyes as he added proudly, "but she is wild and will nowt be tamed."

"Who found her?" Little Fur asked.

"Crow did!" Crow squawked, swooping down. "Crow the Clever was seeing whiteness of vixen in high house in cage. Crow watching and seeing that she was bettering and bettering." He landed and preened himself, adding, "Crow having great cleverness, and best eyes of any bird."

"How is Nobody?" Little Fur asked.

"She cannot walking, and so human laying her

in softed woven basket in sunlight. But Crow can't landing there. Can't talking to vixen."

"I spoke to her," Ginger said quietly. "I told her that we would help her be free as soon as she was healed. But she said she needed no help, for the human had accepted her wildness and meant to free her outside the city when her bones were healed. She said that she would go back to the ice mountains."

Little Fur could not help looking at Sorrow, who said, "I let my pride send Nobody away, but I will nowt be such a fool again. When I heard that she had been hurt and taken by a human, all my cold and canny doubts were swallowed by my fear for her. I saw suddenly that love comes like sunlight at the end of a long winter, and only a great fool would turn from it, claiming to be unworthy. Love is a gift, and once Nobody is free, if she will have me still I will run with her to the ice mountains, or wherever she would run."

"I am so glad," Little Fur said with all her heart.

"Greetings, Healer," said Wander, coming to join them. "You have very interesting friends. It comes to me that merely being your friend is to journey far. If you would permit me, I will visit you in your wilderness."

"I would like that very much," Little Fur said.

Crow interrupted them. "Crow must flying. Must announcing important news of Little Fur's return from the mouth of great sea on the back of a giantful fishiness. Must telling Tillet, and Gem, who is now Sett Owl! Must telling Sly!" As he flapped into the air, his eyes shone with delight at the thought of being the bearer of such important and extraordinary tidings. Little Fur thought that for once, even if he told no more than the exact truth, everyone would believe he exaggerated.

But his words had reminded her of Danger's message. "Where is Sly? Did she go to Underth to spy on the Troll King?"

"She did," said Ginger. "She went and she came back. It was he who sent out the troll Tillet watches over, and a hundred others besides. They were to steal your green stone. Sly said the Troll King desires nothing more than to possess it."

Little Fur's eyes opened wide and she drew a long breath as the answer she had striven for since leaving the deepest green came to her. "I think that he must have what he desires, then."

She looked down at the two stones hanging from her neck and touched her mother's stone with a soft finger. This one she would keep, for it had saved her life through her mother's will. The other, warm to her touch and full of potent and irreplaceable magic, she would give to the small troll. Or perhaps it would be better to allow it to steal the stone and escape, for it would be suspicious of any kindness. Once it got away, it would race triumphantly down to Underth to give the precious stone to the Troll King, who would evoke its power.

The simple perfection of it made her want to laugh.

"Why would you let the Troll King have what he wants?" asked the wander curiously.

"Because, more than anything in the world, I *want* to give him what he wants," said Little Fur, and she burst out laughing. She ran up the sand toward the waving sea grass. She wove through the tufts until she came to brown earth where green grass grew thickly, flecked with purple and yellow flowers. She stopped and at last allowed her yearning to reach down into the earth.

The magic-filled stone hanging from her neck pulsed hot. Earth magic flowed to her feet and up through her body, right to the tips of each furled ear, with such force that she nearly fell over. Little Fur felt herself embraced and filled, all at the same time.

Then the flow of earth magic surged with joy so that the

others all stiffened with surprise at the feel of it.

Oh, clever! You have solved the riddle! The moment the Troll King evokes the stone magic, he will draw me to him in all my strength. To reach him, I must flow through all of his city. The stone pulsed in Little Fur's fingers, and she heard the earth spirit's voice continue. *You know that once you let this stone be taken away, I will never be able to speak to you quite so clearly again?*

Little Fur nodded. "Sometimes a sacrifice is the only way."

Oh, my dearest one, whispered the earth spirit. *I am so proud of you.*

Little Fur smiled and looked around at Sorrow and Ginger. "Let's go home," she said.

ACKNOWLEDGMENTS

Thanks first to my Australian editor, Nan, who understands that editing is not merely correcting but a vital part of the creative process. Thanks also to the wonderful editorial team of Mallory, Chelsea, and Nicholas at Random House in the States, who prove to me that if you are good enough, you can gild the lily. I am lucky to have all of you, because your editing makes me a better writer. Thanks also to Katrina for her burnishing and for telling me about Guerrilla Gardening. Long live all Guerrilla Gardeners!

Heartfelt thanks also to Marina for her wonderful, innovative design skills.

Thanks to the Francouzska Crêperie on Janovského Street in Prague, where I wrote most of this book, and to David and Bernadette, who endured my writing the last of it in their apartment in irresistible Hong Kong. Last but not least, thanks to Gilbert, who let me send the last edited chapter at the last minute from the warm, friendly YHA hostel in Apollo Bay.

ABOUT THE AUTHOR

Isobelle Carmody began the first of her highly acclaimed Obernewtyn Chronicles while she was still in high school, and worked on it while completing a bachelor of arts and then a journalism cadetship. The series and her short stories have established her at the forefront of fantasy writing in Australia.

She has written many award-winning short stories and books for young people. *The Gathering* was a joint winner of the 1993 CBC Book of the Year Award and the 1994 Children's Peace Literature Award. *Billy Thunder and the Night Gate* (published as *Night Gate* in the United States) was short-listed for the Patricia Wrightson Prize for Children's Literature in the 2001 NSW Premier's Literary Awards.

Isobelle divides her time between her homes in Australia and the Czech Republic.